To Cris

from
Mick

Christmas 2014

This is a novel for teenagers
but it's one I really like. Have
read it three or four times and so
will pass it on to you. The sman
really makes the people and the
scenes come alive.

In the

House

of the

Queen's Beasts

Books by Jean Thesman

In the House of the Queen's Beasts

Calling the Swan

The Other Ones

The Tree of Bells

The Moonstones

The Storyteller's Daughter

The Ornament Tree

Summerspell

Cattail Moon

Nothing Grows Here

Molly Donnelly

When the Road Ends

The Rain Catchers

Appointment with a Stranger

Rachel Chance

The Last April Dancers

In the

House

of the

Queen's Beasts

Jean Thesman

VIKING

VIKING
Published by the Penguin Group
Penguin Putnam Inc., 345 Hudson Street, New York, New York 10014, U.S.A.
Penguin Books Ltd, 27 Wrights Lane, London W8 5TZ, England
Penguin Books Australia Ltd, Ringwood, Victoria, Australia
Penguin Books Canada Ltd, 10 Alcorn Avenue, Toronto, Ontario, Canada M4V 3B2
Penguin Books (N.Z.) Ltd, 182-190 Wairau Road, Auckland 10, New Zealand

Penguin Books Ltd, Registered Offices: Harmondsworth, Middlesex, England

1 3 5 7 9 10 8 6 4 2

LIBRARY OF CONGRESS CATALOGING-IN-PUBLICATION DATA
Thesman, Jean.
In the house of the Queen's beasts / Jean Thesman.
p. cm.
Summary: Fourteen-year-old Emily finds refuge in a tree house in the
yard of her new home in Seattle and develops a friendship with a troubled girl.

ISBN 0-670-89285-8 (hc)

[1. Friendship—Fiction. 2. Self-perception—Fiction. 3. Family problems—Fiction.
4. Stepfamilies—Fiction. 5. Moving, Household—Fiction. 6. Tree houses—Fiction.
7. Seattle (Wash.)—Fiction.]   I. Title.

PZ7.T3525 In 2001

[Fic]—dc21   00-040816

Printed in the U.S.A.
Set in Berkeley

For Athena and Maggie

Sometimes, in the last weeks we'd lived in our other house, my nightmares would wake me and I'd get up to look in the bedroom mirror. I'd always expect to see the scar, but my new face would stare back at me, and then I'd lean closer to examine the too-smooth skin on my cheek.

The people I'd known in middle school would see the change, but the people I had yet to meet would never suspect that I'd once looked quite different. Or so my parents said.

I'd go back to bed and try to sleep, but in my imagination, I'd relive the accident again, and run after the Frisbee again, and stumble again.

And hear the glass shatter again.

Moving from one house to another was hard work, and after I'd carried the third box of pans into the remodeled kitchen, I stopped for a drink of cold water. There were so many of us that we were getting in each other's ways. They could spare me for a few minutes.

I opened the kitchen door and sipped from the glass we'd all been sharing, while I looked out over the deck to the long backyard. The unmowed grass had bent and silvered under the chilly rain that poured down while the graduate students Dad had hired carried in our upholstered furniture. Now that we were down to boxes of books and kitchen stuff, the rain had stopped. Wouldn't you know it?

I walked outside in the gray-green of the early June afternoon. Everything was quiet, and the world felt poised, as if something were about to happen. I had seen the yard earlier from the windows in the kitchen and my bedroom. It was sheltered with big trees and divided into irregular sections by overgrown flower beds. The tree house was visible through the low-hanging branches of a giant maple.

The old people who had lived here had told us that there was a tree house, but I hadn't been curious about it until today. I was fourteen, after all, past the age where a playhouse in a tree meant much. All things considered, I was so relieved to move from our old neighborhood that I would have been satisfied in a cave, as long as it was out of the reach of my enemies.

"Emily, are you going to stand out there all day?" Grady asked.

My brother was eighteen, had just graduated from high school, and had spent the day being insufferably bossy.

"Coming," I groaned, and I closed the new glass door behind me. He had stacked another box on top of the boxes I had already put on the counter. "Where's C.J.?" I asked. "Lying down on the couch again?"

He ignored my comment. "This place is as drafty as an old barn," he said. "And it's cold. . . ."

"Dad turned off the furnace because we're leaving the front door open while people go in and out," I argued.

"And the stairs creak. . . ." he went on doggedly.

"What is it with you and this house?" I demanded. "You've been complaining ever since you found out Mom and Dad bought it."

He rubbed his curly dark hair with one dirty paw. "I liked the other house." He looked vaguely embarrassed for a moment, and then he scowled at me and said, "We'd lived there since I was seven. I knew where everything was."

"I don't see what difference it makes to you," I said. "You'll be staying in a dorm after September. Why don't you grow up?"

But he was already heading out, no doubt going back to one

of the trucks parked in the driveway of the big old house I already loved as much as my parents did. The place was roomy and filled with natural light, and it smelled faintly of dust and cinnamon potpourri. The people who had lived in it for fifty years had left behind nothing but wonderful feelings—and a well-worn dog collar dangling a tag engraved with the name Stubby. Their family had been happy here. We would be, too.

Dad came in then, carrying a box Mom had marked "cans." He put it down next to the sink and helped himself to the last of the chocolate chip cookies one of his students had brought for everyone. "Grady just passed me, looking grim. Have you two been arguing again?"

"He keeps on and on about the house. He's even got C.J. doing it. This is the best house I ever saw, and I'd want to be here even if I . . ." I was going to say, "Even if I hadn't hated where we lived before," but I didn't. Dad already knew that.

"I'll bear your affection for the place in mind after I've been struck blind by the bills from two contractors, the furnace man, and the plumber who still insists that his truck was dented by my parked car." He rubbed the top of his balding head and sighed. "Have you seen C.J.?"

"Did you look under the piano?" I asked sarcastically. "In the hall closet? He seems to need places to hide so he can rest in peace after all the work he's done watching the rest of us carry boxes."

Grady came in then, and dropped an armload of his clothes on a kitchen chair. C.J. Sanderson shambled in behind him, empty-handed as usual. As far as I knew, he hadn't helped all morning. But he sure had plenty to say about our new home, and most of it was critical. Grady hadn't told him to shut up, either, and I was longing to accept that responsibility myself. I was sure that C.J. was jealous of us.

"Hey, Emily, did you see the scratch marks on the inside of the front door?" C.J. asked. "Looks like somebody got locked inside this old barn and tried to escape."

Old barn? Didn't he see Dad standing there? I longed to sock C.J. but instead, I asked, "Why don't you help us out? You're getting paid for it, aren't you?"

C.J. scowled at me from under his blond eyebrows and slipped out through the door to the hall.

Grady pretended he didn't notice the exchange, and he leaned against the counter next to Dad. "Did I hear somebody talking about a car when I came in?"

"We're talking about bills right now," Dad said. "Comments about cars at this time would be ill-advised. Trust me." He turned on the sink faucet and splashed water over his face. "Mumble mumble," he continued, as he rubbed his face with his sleeve.

"Paper towels, Dad," I said, handing him a roll I took out of one of the boxes someone had carried in earlier.

"Getting me a used car would cost less than heating this warehouse for a week," Grady complained.

I looked over my shoulder at him. "In September, think about all the space we have while you're sharing a room with somebody who snores and stores his dirty underwear in his desk drawers." I laughed rudely at my own joke, just to make sure he got my point.

"Yeah, yeah," Grady said. He ran upstairs to his new room with his clothes, and then came back down to help the other guys.

Dad had hired not only two of his graduate students but also three of their friends, and none of them had ever moved anything bigger than a box of books before. "They need the money," he had told Mom, who was suspicious of any plan that involved amateurs. C.J. had manipulated himself into the deal, too, but I intended to complain about him at payoff time. Maybe I'd be lucky enough to embarrass him.

Mom had moved her good china herself, with help from nice, reliable me, the day before. She had hired specialists to move the piano on Friday.

A crash in the living room shook the house. "You'd better stay out of the way now, Emily," Dad told me when he finished wiping himself dry. "The guys are a little clumsy. You can help with the unpacking later on."

Happy to oblige, I went outside again, down the deck steps and into the big yard. I loved working in flower gardens and so did Mom. We planned on having wonderful times out here.

I ducked under the drooping branches of a dogwood tree and followed the narrow path that wound between flower beds, finally stopping at six wooden steps that had been nailed to the trunk of the great, spreading maple.

The tree house looked like a tower that had been removed from the house and placed in the backyard. It, too, was made of dark timber and stucco, and both looked as if they had been transplanted from England. If the playhouse had been higher up, it could have been the tower where Rapunzel had been held captive.

In spite of my age, the little house charmed me. I climbed the steps and ducked my head as I walked through the low doorway.

"Hello," a voice said tentatively, on a rising note, almost like a timid question.

I nearly fell backward out the door. "Who are you?" I exclaimed, my heart pounding.

A girl sat on a low bench, her hands folded in her lap, her round, freckled face anxious. "I'm Rowan Tucker," she said. "I live back there." She turned on the bench and pointed out the big window. "In the house behind you. The people who lived here, the Bonners, let me use the tree house, but then they said you were coming and that I wasn't supposed to be here without your permission, but I didn't know it would be so soon, so I came over to get my things, but then the movers came, and I was sort of stuck here and . . ." Her voice trailed off. She pushed her thick glasses back up her small nose. "Sorry," she said. "I'm talking too much. I'll get my stuff and go."

The room was larger than I'd thought, six-sided, with two windows and a built-in bench under each one. I watched Rowan try to roll up a set of carving tools in a strip of faded purple flannel, but half of them slipped out of her hands and clattered to the floor among a light scattering of wood shavings. Grady had a set of tools like hers, but not nearly as nice.

Rowan was shorter than I and dressed in baggy jeans and an oversize T-shirt that looked as if they belonged to someone else. Her dark brown hair was rumpled, as if she had been running her fingers through it instead of combing it.

I was embarrassed, catching someone trespassing. I stood there uncertainly, trying to think of something to say that wouldn't hurt her feelings or anger her, but wouldn't be too friendly, either, to establish that we, the Shepherds, lived in the house now, and the tree house was mine.

On each side of the doorway, a narrow shelf held wooden carvings. There were several on each side, so I pretended to look them over while she fumbled with her carving tools, but I couldn't concentrate.

"Did you make these?" I asked.

"Yes," she said. She added, "They aren't very good."

"They're fine," I said hastily as I leaned close to study the one nearest the door on the left side. It was clearly a whale, but she was right—it was rather rough. Next to it sat a bear, and next to that, an elephant. Each one had been carved so that it looked as if it stood on a pedestal.

"They're the Queen's Beasts," she said.

I turned to look at her. "What?" I wasn't sure I'd heard her right.

She laughed a little, as if she was embarrassed. She had rolled the tools up successfully at last. "I named them that because of the Queen's Beasts in England. Have you seen them? They're in London, in a wonderful garden. The tree house reminds me of houses in England. When I started carving, I thought about the Queen's Beasts and I wished I could see them again." She stopped. I think she realized that I had no idea what she was talking about.

I blinked and looked away. "Oh," was all I could think of saying. Then I had a great inspiration and added, "I've never been to England, but my parents have. They went there on their honeymoon, but they left Grady and me behind with Grady's grandparents." Then I realized what I had just said and how weird it sounded, and I blushed miserably. I had been three when my mother married seven-year-old Grady's father, but we were all one family now.

Rowan cleared her throat. "Well, maybe they saw the Queen's Beasts," she said. "You could ask them."

In the silence that was much too long, she began taking the little wooden figures down and shoving them into a grimy blue striped pillowcase.

"Don't," I said impulsively. "You can leave them, if you want. You can come here, just like you always did. It's okay."

She didn't look up, but she shook her head. "I can't. The Bonners said I had to have your family's permission. I shouldn't have been here today."

"But I just gave you permission," I said. What more did she want?

"Your parents—your mother or . . ."

Well, I had asked for that one, with my blurting out our family circumstances.

"My parents wouldn't mind," I said. "After all, this is my tree house. I get to pick who comes inside."

She sat back down, clearly amazed. "Are you sure?" she asked.

"Positive," I said. Then I remembered that she didn't know who I was. "I'm Emily Shepherd," I said. "I've got a brother named Grady and a dog named Daisy. She's staying with my aunt today."

Rowan nodded. "The Bonners said that your mother is a doctor and your father teaches history at the university."

"Right," I said, and then I waited. This was the time to exchange information, part of a kind of dance people do when they first meet. But, strangely, Rowan said nothing about her family. She took the animals out of the pillowcase and set them carefully on the shelf, in the same order they had been in before.

I was desperate to fill up the silence. "Where do you go to school?" I asked. I didn't know her age for sure and guessed that she might be a year or so behind me since she was smaller. "I'll be starting ninth grade in the fall."

"Hey, so will I," Rowan said, grinning. "We can take the bus to high school together."

I grinned back. But then I remembered my face—was she looking at it?—and turned the good right side to her as I pretended to examine the Queen's Beasts again.

But my face was fine now, I told myself firmly.

". . . and you'll like Lorna and Carlene," Rowan was saying. "They live six blocks from here, but they're my best friends."

I nodded, wondering what they'd be like. Meeting Rowan had been easy. She was just *here,* like the tree house and Queen's Beasts. But now that I was on the verge of meeting two more girls, I was filled with that awful anxious feeling that I hated so much.

"Emily!" That was Mom, bellowing from the back door. "Where are you?"

"Here!" I bellowed back. "In the tree house!"

"I've ordered in pizza for everybody!" Mom shouted. "Come on in."

I realized then that Rowan looked horrified, probably at our shouting. Well, that was the Shepherd family. We communicated, as Dad said, with many layers of enthusiasm.

"Do you want to eat with us?" I asked Rowan. "Mom always orders too much. Then you can meet my family and the guys who helped us move."

"The movers?" she asked. She clearly had been uncomfortable while Mom and I were exchanging bellows, and my invitation seemed to take her by surprise. She brushed wood shavings into a neat little pile and put them in her pocket.

"No, they're really some of my dad's students," I said. "He hired them instead of regular movers. They're funny and nice. Come on."

"I'd better not. It's getting late, and my parents wouldn't like me making a pest of myself."

"You're not a pest," I said.

But she thanked me again—twice, actually—for letting her leave her Queen's Beasts in the tree house and climbed down the steps quickly. I watched her disappear through the trees, then reappear as she climbed easily over a tall wooden fence at the back of our yard, as if she'd done it a million times.

"Emily!" Grady yelled. "For Pete's sake, hurry up!"

I hoped Rowan hadn't heard that, but there wasn't much chance she could have missed it. Grady could be heard for miles. I took one more look around at the wood-paneled walls, stained with age, and the thick plank floor that needed a good cleaning—and the Queen's Beasts, standing side by side on their shelves, watching me with what I thought was approval. This would be a great place to think. And talk with a friend.

I scrambled down the steps and ran to the deck.

"We're ready to eat," Mom said as I came in the kitchen. "Help me carry in the glasses." She looked tired—and happier than she had been for a long time. Why not? We had moved into the house we had wanted for years.

"I met the girl who lives behind us," I said. "Her name is Rowan. She's been using the tree house."

"That must be the girl the Bonners told me about," Mom said as she bumped open the swinging door to the dining room with her hip. "Did you like her?"

"Yes," I said. "We're in the same grade."

"Good," Mom said. "Now you'll have somebody to show you the ropes."

Dad's students and their friends were already sitting at the long table talking about cars with Grady, and Dad was opening pizza boxes on the buffet. Darn it, I had missed seeing Dad pay everybody. His checkbook was lying next to his plate—and smirking C.J. was tucking a check into his shirt pocket. I loathed him! He hadn't earned a cent.

"It's a good thing we set this room up right away," Dad said, pleased with himself as he looked around at the beautiful paneled walls and our own furniture, which looked better here than it had in our old house. "I'm glad we're having our first meal in the dining room with friends."

"I hope you guys put up the beds," Mom said as she passed

out paper plates and glasses. C.J. helped himself to milk first, before anyone else could reach the carton.

"Oh, beds," one of the students said, wincing and looking about at the others. "We meant to do it."

"We were too busy hauling around all that heavy stuff," C.J. said.

"Yeah," I said rudely. "I saw you taking a rest on the living room couch as soon as somebody else moved it in."

Grady choked, coughed, excused himself, and then presented me with one of his best dirty looks.

"We can handle the beds ourselves," Dad said. I'd heard Mom's sigh, even if he had not. She was really tired.

My room overlooked the backyard and had a dressing room with a small window from which I had a view of a squirrel's messy nest in a pine tree. My mattress and box spring sat on the floor, and my rolled-up bedding had been dumped on top. The sun was going down, not that I could see it from any of my windows, but the sky above the trees was the color of slate and there were no shadows on the grass under the trees. Our first evening in our new home.

I flopped down on the mattress and hugged myself. We wouldn't have been in the house if Mrs. Bonner's middle-aged daughter had not been Mom's patient. That was how we learned that it was being sold.

Grady stuck his head in the door to tell me that C.J. and the guys had left and he'd help me put up my bed if I wanted. "Dad's gone to get Daisy and Mom's lying down in the living room," he went on. Then he added, "What do you think of the house now?"

I sat up. "I really like it," I said. "It's big though. Seven bedrooms. I practically get lost looking for a bathroom."

"It's just the right size for a family of elephants," he said. "Three bedrooms for the family, one guest room, Dad's library, Mom's office—and a room for the spiders. There must be a hundred of them here. Do you want me to help you with your bed or not, kid?"

"Not," I said. "I'm comfortable just like this. Maybe you can help me later."

"Nope," he said on his way out the door. "I'm going to be busy hooking up the TV sets and computers."

A few minutes later, Dad returned and carried Daisy upstairs to me. "She won't climb the stairs," he said as he put my small old brown and white dog down beside me on the mattress. "She says she doesn't do stairs, at least not strange stairs."

"She'll love it here," I predicted, as Daisy washed my face and made herself comfortable next to me on the mattress. "I'll show her the tree house."

"You like that, do you?" Dad said. "I thought you might."

"Do you remember statues in England called the Queen's Beasts?" I asked.

He looked up at the ceiling, thought for a moment, then said, "You'd better ask your mother. We saw maybe a million statues. She knows more about art than I do. Why do you ask?"

"The girl who lives behind us—Rowan—she carved little

animals and lined them up on shelves in the tree house. She calls them the Queen's Beasts. She's been to England."

"Your mom collected guidebooks everywhere," he said. "If we saw these Beasts, she's got a guidebook tucked away or maybe some snapshots. Now, do you want me to set up your bed?"

I shook my head. "I can wait until tomorrow. Daisy and I are just fine here."

"Come downstairs in a while, though. I bought some ice cream—chocolate for you, mocha for Grady, and strawberry for your mother."

I sat up and leaned on one elbow. "What about you?"

"Oh, they're *all* fine with me," he said.

Daisy was already asleep, snuggled against my legs. I scratched her curly brown ears and looked around. Mom had promised that she and I would pick out new wallpaper as soon as they could afford it, but I wanted what was already there. The small, faded pink roses on a cream background suited the room and the house. And me.

Our "movers" had put the mirror back on my dresser, and before I went downstairs, I examined my face carefully. I could see where the scar had been—or I thought I could. The skin there was smooth, almost shiny, and too perfect. The notch on the bridge of my nose had been almost completely repaired, but I could still feel it under my fingertips.

I dipped my head so that my blunt cut brown hair fell over my left cheek. There wasn't much to hide, not really. Dad had been right when he'd said, "There's nothing wrong anymore. You're a pretty girl, Emily. The bad times are over."

"Unless I run into someone who knows me," I had said. "Someone who remembers Scarface."

He had put his hands on my shoulders and said, "Miss Emily Shepherd is big enough to pity the people who can't get out of a ditch unless they've pulled someone down to step on."

My dad was a good man. My luckiest day was the day Mom married him.

I heard a TV set blare down the hall. Grady had hooked his TV up to cable and was watching wrestling. Daisy, snoring lightly, stirred and lay still again.

We were home.

Before I went downstairs, I looked out my window again and saw a light shining through the misty yard. That must be Rowan's house, I thought.

I carried groggy Daisy downstairs and we all ate ice cream in the kitchen.

"How about looking at cars tomorrow after I get home from work?" Grady asked Dad. His dark curly head was bent over his ice cream as he tried to pretend he didn't really care all that much.

"Tomorrow?" Dad said, helping himself to more chocolate ice cream. "You're starting college tomorrow? Where could the summer have gone?"

"I thought we could get it early," Grady said. Now he looked up, his bright hazel eyes fixed on Dad. "You know, so I could get used to it over the summer."

"You're used to my car," Dad said. "You're used to your mother's car. That's enough for now."

"Dad!" Grady protested. "Everybody—"

"Didn't just buy a house they couldn't really afford," Dad said cheerfully. "I might see my way clear to getting the car for you in six weeks or so, if you save enough of your salary this summer."

"Save?" Grady asked bleakly, as if he'd never heard the word before.

"It's what we poor slaves do," Mom said, and she licked her spoon. "We work and save. But I don't see the harm if you two start looking around for a really cheap deal."

"Can I go, too?" I asked.

"Nope," Grady said. He had mocha ice cream on his upper lip, which I was happy to tell him about.

"I'll be needing you here to help me in the evenings," Mom told me. "I can't let Grady or your father help with closets because they think throwing clothing on a floor is good enough. Now, folks, I'm going to take a shower and go to bed."

Daisy and I slept under a jumble of blankets until the part of the night that I always called Middle Dark. Something outside woke Daisy, who sat up and barked shrilly several times. I didn't hear anything, but she wouldn't settle down, so I got up and turned on the overhead light.

"Everybody okay?" Dad asked outside my door. Daisy stopped barking and whined instead.

"Daisy heard something outside, but I didn't," I said.

"Everything's locked up," he said. "But maybe I'll go down and have a look around."

I heard him go downstairs, move around on the first floor, open the back door, and finally come upstairs again.

"There's nothing in the house that shouldn't be here, and I didn't see anything unusual outside, either," he reported at my door.

"Maybe Daisy's just worried about all the different neighborhood sounds," I said. I turned out the light and Daisy and I settled back on the mattress.

But there would come a time when Daisy's Middle Dark alarms would keep me awake for the rest of the night. There would come a time when I knew what worried my old dog.

Chapter 2

Monday morning I woke when I heard Grady leave in Dad's car for his summer job with a landscaping company. A few minutes later, Mom left in her SUV for hospital rounds. The house was serene, and Daisy snored gently at my feet.

Shower water began running in the new bathroom next to my parents' room, so I knew Dad was up. I yawned and stretched, thought about getting up, and changed my mind. Grady had probably left a mess in the bathroom I had to share with him. Maybe I'd use the small bathroom connected to the guest room.

We'd owned the house for many weeks, but so much work had to be done in it that it hadn't been ready until the first day of May. The upstairs bathrooms and the small half-bath downstairs had been remodeled, along with the kitchen. We chose new carpet for downstairs, and the wood floors in the bedrooms had been refinished. We still didn't move in May, though, because Grady was graduating from high school in a month.

But I would have changed schools in a minute. I had hated my middle school, where I had walked alone in the halls, sat alone in the cafeteria, and kept my head down, even after the second surgery that had finally repaired my face.

I heard Dad whistling as he went downstairs, so I got up and pushed back my heavy old cream silk curtains. The sky was almost clear, with only a straggling line of thin white clouds far away. Daisy barked at my closed door and our day began.

Dad made my breakfast, which, he said, was the last thing he planned to do for me that day. "We'll put up the beds and try to get organized around here. I'm counting on you to eat whenever you're hungry."

I spread jam on toast and said, "I have a strong hunch that Mom doesn't want you unpacking boxes without her supervision. You fling things around."

"Oh, I wouldn't unpack a box," he assured me. "I'll fling the big stuff around until everything looks right. I wish I'd let the boys move the piano. I know they could have done it. Professional piano movers! That cost a fortune! Bah."

I finished my juice in four big sour gulps. "I liked coming in yesterday and seeing the piano already there in the alcove, like a welcoming committee."

Dad rinsed out his coffee cup and put it in the new dishwasher. "You've already made a friend, too."

"Well, Rowan's sort of a friend. I hardly know her. I forgot to ask Mom about the Queen's Beasts, though. Where would she have put the guidebooks?"

"I can never find anything that she puts away, and moving didn't enlighten me. Ask her when she gets back tonight."

We put up the beds and did out best to make the bedrooms look nice, although we knew Mom would arrange everything when she got home. Dad left me to deal with clothes and closets. At noon I went to the kitchen to make a sandwich and found that Dad had been there before me. The milk carton was sitting on the counter and the milk was already lukewarm.

The kitchen was under my bedroom, so I looked out the window over the sink, hoping to see my tree house, but the tall rhododendrons hid it. I could fix a quick lunch and eat it in the tree house, I thought. I gathered up a banana, a handful of bakery cookies, and a cold bottle of lemonade. Daisy, who had been following me from room to room, scampered out the back door behind me.

When we reached the tree house, I put down the food so I could boost Daisy up the steps. By the time I reached the door, she was sniffing around inside, wagging her stump of a tail. She liked the place. Well, who wouldn't?

I'd had a small hope that Rowan would be there, but she wasn't. Her big brick house almost appeared to be rearing up on a sharp rise of ground on the other side of the fence, and I could see the windows with their closed blinds. I couldn't tell if anyone was home. Goosebumps rose on my arms. I didn't know why, but I didn't like the look of that house. The bare bricks were too dark and the house was too square and bulky. It looked like a prison. Weren't people supposed to plant ivy on brick houses?

The Queen's Beasts sat in their two straight rows and seemed to invite me to touch them. I picked up the whale first, and then the horse. When I looked closely, I saw that both of them were smiling. All of the animals were smiling!

What a strange girl Rowan was.

Daisy liked the place—her tail never stopped wagging. But as soon as I finished eating, I carried her and my garbage down the steps and headed back to the house.

"Couldn't resist, could you?" Dad asked as I stepped into the kitchen. "Maybe I'll have to visit the tree house myself."

"Only if I invite you," I said. "I'm the boss there."

He threw up his hands. "That sounds like something Grady would say."

"Nothing I say is like something Grady would say these days," I said as I threw my garbage into the trash can under the sink. "What is it with him? He's been such a big pain for the last few months."

"He's trying out various personalities," Dad said. "Feel free to defend yourself at any time."

"Maybe he's trying to grow up fast so he doesn't miss us when he starts at the university in the fall and lives in a dorm," I said.

Dad rubbed my scalp with his knuckles. "Would you like to teach a 'Truth about Teenagers' seminar this summer?" he asked, laughing.

By mid-afternoon I needed another time-out in the tree house. I had hoped Rowan would be there, and that time she was. My smile was probably much too big to be cool.

"Working again?" I asked, when I saw her put a sharp knife down on the bench.

She held up a block of wood with a rough shape scratched into it. "I'm carving a unicorn," she said. "If it turns out right, I'll give it to you. If you want, that is."

"Sure, I do," I said. I sat down on the bench facing her. "Why did you pick a unicorn?"

"You look like somebody who might like unicorns," she said. She picked up her knife and scratched at the wood again.

Unicorns were all right, but I'd never given them much thought. I didn't seem to have much of an imagination. However, I didn't want to hurt Rowan's feelings, so I said, "You're right."

"Are you all unpacked now?" she asked, bending over the wood.

"No, not really. I thought we'd be done by now, but there's still a big pile of stuff in the hall. Do you want to come in? The house is a mess, but you could get an idea of what it will be like when we're finished."

"I'd love to, but I can't. Not unless your parents say it's all right."

I stared at Rowan, who didn't look up from the block of wood. Mom and Dad didn't care if I invited someone to come in the house—not that I had for the last two years. They might be surprised, but they wouldn't complain. They didn't even complain about C.J., at least not where I could hear them.

"I know it would be all right, but I'll ask them anyway," I said. "Then you can come in."

Did she wait too long to say something? Was there a tension in the tree house now that was so strong I not only felt it but could almost hear it?

"If they call my parents—*someday*—and everybody says it's all right," Rowan said in a tight little voice.

"Sure, they can do that," I said brightly, as if I didn't already suspect that Mom and Dad would find this whole thing as strange as I did. Time to change the subject. "I like your name," I said. "I've never heard it before."

"I was named after my English grandmother," she said. She folded up her knife and slipped it into her pocket, then rubbed the block of wood on her jeans. "I'll work on this again tomorrow," she said. "I don't like to finish things too soon. Just soon enough."

Another silence hung over us. I wracked my brain trying to think of something else to say and wished I'd brought my dog with me. Daisy was always worth talking about.

"Do you like to read?" Rowan asked as she arranged the unfinished unicorn on a shelf.

"Sure," I said. I could talk about books forever. "What's your all-time favorite book?"

Rowan had taken off her glasses, and she blinked as if she couldn't see too well. "I like fantasy and science fiction, and everything else, so the last book I read is always my favorite."

I laughed. "I know how you feel. What's your favorite TV program?"

She shook her head. "We don't watch much TV. Sometimes we see movies, if they don't have violence or sex in them." She put her glasses back on and added, "I wear contacts most of the time, but I'm not supposed to when I'm carving. Something might get in my eyes."

"That would hurt," I said.

"What's *your* favorite TV program?" she asked. She seemed to be more than just polite. She actually seemed interested.

"I like nature programs," I said. "But Mom calls television 'brain poison.'"

"So she doesn't watch?" Rowan asked.

"Only every single night," I said, grinning.

We both laughed then. Rowan's green eyes flashed through curly black lashes, and I realized that she was prettier than I'd thought. Did she know it? Was she one of those girls who compared herself with everybody else? Where would I rank in her mind, with my scars—no, with my repaired skin? My slightly nicked nose?

"I'd better go," she said. "It's almost time for my parents to get home from work. I'm supposed to clean the living room today, since I didn't do it yesterday. It looks fine, but you know how it goes."

I didn't know, actually. In our family, the house was clean if we could walk from one room to another without tripping over something.

But I said, "I know."

She grinned, almost cautiously. "Those vacuum cleaner marks have to line up straight with the walls," she said. "That's how Dad likes them."

I stifled a shocked laugh. "You bet," I said. "They'd better be straight."

She slipped past me and went quickly down the steps. "See you tomorrow, maybe," she said.

"Tomorrow," I agreed. I watched her run to the fence, and I saw for the first time the tall wooden box that she used to boost herself to the top. Who had put the box there for her? The former owners of my house, probably. They must have really liked her.

I liked her, too. But she belonged in another time, when people were more formal, and everybody needed permission for everything. I'd seen historical movies where the girls and young women didn't have real lives, but just waited for something to happen to them instead of going out and making it happen. Was Rowan like that, waiting for something to happen and not having any control over it?

Suddenly Daisy yapped at the foot of the steps, and I stuck my head out the door and told her I'd be right down. I looked around the tree house once more and wondered if I should fix up the little place. What about cushions for the benches and a rug for the floor?

Mom had a big stack of decorating magazines and I was sure I could persuade her to invest a little money in the tree house, especially since I didn't want any changes in my bedroom. What fun!

Mom brought Chinese food home and we were setting the kitchen table when Grady came in, dirty and smelling like cedar chips.

"At least wash your hands," Mom said, glancing at him. "And not in the sink, if you please."

"Aww . . ." Grady began.

"Wash."

He ran out of the room and Daisy ran after him, barking. Dad, pouring water in tall glasses, said, "Doesn't Daisy recognize him either? I'm not surprised. What does he do to get so dirty?"

"Don't joke about it," Mom said. "I want him to respect his job—and save his money."

I sat down and unfolded my napkin. "Rowan was in the tree house this afternoon. The benches are really hard. I'd like to have cushions and maybe a rug. What do you think, Mom?"

"Cute," Mom said. She slid into the chair next to me. "I like the idea of decorating the tree house. After dinner, I'll come and take a look."

Grady came back, slightly cleaner. "I'm starved," he said, and he reached for the carton of sweet-and-sour pork. "I haven't eaten since the two o'clock break. Hey, Emily, we're fixing up a yard north of town, and one of the guys found some bones in a flower bed. Maybe human bones. That house was an old house, too, just like this one."

"So you called the police," Mom said flatly. "If you really think they're human bones and you didn't call the police and show them the bones, you'll be in trouble."

"Aw, Mom, it's a joke," Grady protested.

"You give me the creeps," I said, as I took a second helping of fried rice.

"Family dinners," Dad said, licking his fingers. "They're the foundation of civilization."

"Last time, you said that indoor plumbing was the foundation of civilization," Grady argued as he emptied the last of the pork out of the carton.

———

After dinner, while Grady and Dad cleaned the kitchen, Mom went out to the tree house with me and looked around. "I love this," she said. "It's exactly what I would have wanted when I was a kid. But you're right. It needs something. A good cleaning, for starters."

"And cushions for the benches and a rug on the floor," I said. "I'd rather fix this place up than my bedroom."

"It needs paint, too," she said. "These walls are ugly. Hey, I like these cute shelves. And look at the little animals!"

"Rowan calls them the Queen's Beasts, after some statues she saw when she was in London."

"I remember them!" Mom said. "I took snapshots of them. I'll dig them out tonight—no, in a few days." She looked around again. "I really love this place. I'll get Dad to take you shopping for things. He won't complain—much—as long as you don't want anything done to your room. Maybe Rowan could go with you. She's artistic—she probably has lots of ideas."

"I'll ask her next time I see her," I said.

"Oh, call her up this evening," Mom said. "I'm excited about this."

"I don't know her phone number." I felt strangely reluctant to call Rowan, and I wasn't sure why. Perhaps it was the memory of those blank windows at her house. And a father who wanted her to leave vacuum cleaner marks side by side on the carpet.

"Then just run over and ask her," Mom said.

I hesitated a little too long.

She looked at me sharply. "What's wrong, Emily?"

I shrugged, trying to look casual, but Mom was always a block ahead of me.

"Am I going to hate this or am I going to *really* hate this?" she asked.

"When I asked Rowan to come in and meet you, she said she couldn't go in the house, not unless you called her parents first and got their permission. So I don't think I want to just knock on their door. They sound sort of . . . I don't know. But Rowan's nice! She really is."

"Her parents are just cautious," Mom said reasonably. "That's good. We can't be too careful about our children. But still . . ." She stopped and looked out the window toward Rowan's house. "What a bleak place! Maybe knocking on their door isn't such a good idea." She shook her head and ruffled up her short blond hair. "Listen to me! This is ridiculous! Her parents are worried about us and now I'm worried about them. Tell you what. Next time you see her, ask her if she wants to go shopping with you and Dad, and if she needs permission, he can stroll around the block to their house and tell them the plan. How's that?"

"I thought maybe he could just climb over the fence, like she does," I said, laughing.

Mom grinned. "Now that's a picture I don't want to dwell on too long."

She left, and I looked around the tree house. It needed a red carpet, one with flowers on it. And flowered cushions, deep and soft. But what color should the walls be? I needed to look through some magazines.

I lost track of time that night. I had a dozen magazines on my bed, along with Daisy, and I was still turning pages and comparing things when I realized that it was one-thirty. Middle Dark. I got out of bed, stacked the magazines on my dresser, and was about to turn out the light when Daisy raised her head, stared at the window, and barked.

"What do you hear?" I asked.

Daisy barked sharply twice more.

I turned out the light and opened the curtains. It took my eyes a moment to adjust to the dark, and then I dimly saw the trees in the yard, their leaves fluttering a little in a light breeze, showing silver undersides.

Daisy raised up on her back feet and looked out the window, too. She growled faintly, then got down and jumped back on my bed. Whatever she'd heard must have gone away.

I closed the curtains and got into bed. I was uneasy and so cold that I was shivering.

That was the second night in a row that Daisy had heard something that disturbed her. But I hadn't heard anything at all. I knew that dogs could hear better than people. But what was in our backyard that upset her? The night before, Dad had looked outside and hadn't seen anything.

Maybe it's only a raccoon or possum, I told myself. We had the kind of backyard that would attract them. That must be it.

I hadn't been asleep very long when Daisy burst into yelps and shrieks. I sat up, terrified, holding my hands over my mouth to stifle a scream. I could hear something scratching on wood somewhere.

Daisy had gone wild and was throwing herself at the door. I turned on the bedside light but I was too frightened to get up.

"Grady!" Dad yelled.

I got up then, furious, and yanked open the door. Grady, on his hands and knees by my door, was laughing. Daisy darted at him and licked his face.

"What's going on!" Dad bellowed.

Grady scrambled to his feet. "I was only scratching on her door for a joke, Dad."

"Joke?" Dad shouted. "I practically had a heart attack!"

Mom came out of the room, tying her robe. "Grady, if you come out of your bedroom once more before six-thirty, I'm fining you twenty dollars."

"Twenty dollars!" Grady cried. "Are you kidding?"

"That's the going price for teasing your sister," Mom said.

"Do I get the money?" I asked happily.

Mom glared.

"That's a no, right?" I asked.

"Go back to bed," Mom told me.

"All I want is a little peace," Dad grumbled as he shuffled back to bed.

"Crybaby," Grady whispered to me.

"Jerk," I whispered back.

My heart was still beating too hard when I shut my door. I left the light on for the rest of the night. Grady!

When I slept, I dreamed of Rowan's Queen's Beasts, circling my house and guarding me. Or was it Rowan's house they guarded?

The dream woke me up for a while. I felt that tension again that was almost a sound and too high to hear. I patted Daisy until she sighed and moved out of reach. Was I too old to take a teddy bear to bed with me? I wasn't afraid of the dark, just nightmares.

But I was afraid of Rowan's blind and brooding house.

I fell asleep again and began the terrible dream I'd had many times after my accident. I knew I was dreaming, but I was helpless and couldn't stop. I saw the blue Frisbee coming toward me, wobbling a little, glinting in the bright sunlight, and I moved backward quickly, turned, jumped—and fell.

Glass splintered, sounding no more dangerous than the snap of ice cracking on a shallow puddle, but it would change my life and rob me of my courage. Emily, the best grade school soccer player, was now afraid to run up the stairs.

I woke up again, touching the left side of my face, expecting to feel the thick rope of scar tissue that had run from the bridge of my nose to my earlobe. In the dark, I reached for Daisy, and perhaps she knew what I had dreamed, because she was snuggled against me and licked my new face.

Things will be different now, I told myself. At my new school, there won't be anyone around who remembers me as "Scarface." Nobody who would rather not be seen with me in public. Nobody to remember what I looked like when my face was covered with bandages and it hurt me so much to talk that I simply stopped.

Chapter 3

The sun was shining Tuesday morning when I woke. For a moment I'd thought I was still in our old house, but when I saw the delicate, faded wallpaper I'd already grown to love, I caught myself smiling.

On the way down to the kitchen, I admired everything I passed. It was as if I wanted the house to know how much I appreciated it. I loved the heavy dark woodwork, so elaborately carved, and the high cove ceilings, and the brass carpet rods on the wide stairs. I loved the tall cut-glass windows downstairs and the marble fireplace with the decorated tile inserts and the polished brass screen. It was a house built for families. It was home now.

When I reached the kitchen, Mom and Grady were still there, finishing breakfast at the counter. I let Daisy out the kitchen door and watched while she ran around the yard, nose down in the tall grass.

"When is somebody going to cut the grass?" I asked.

"I'm not cutting it," Grady said, definitely. "We'll need to borrow equipment from a wheat farmer to take care of it. Or maybe buy a flamethrower."

"You told me you were getting off early today," Mom said. She tasted her instant coffee and made a face. "You said something about not being able to finish work on a place because the sprinkler system wasn't installed yet. You can cut the grass when you get home."

"Mom!" Grady complained. "Can't Dad do it? What about Emily? All she ever does is poke around in flower beds."

"Emily is taking care of the kitchen cupboards today," Mom said. "She remembers to wash her hands and she doesn't break things. Too often. And Dad will be unpacking books."

"I'd rather unpack books," Grady grouched. "I spend all day grubbing in people's yards and getting yelled at. I'd like to do something indoors for a change."

"You've only had the job for two weeks, and look at all the money you earn," I said. "Anyway, you'll be in college in a few months. You ought to be glad to be outside now, getting a tan. The girls will love it."

That brightened his mood, but he didn't want to admit it. However, he went off smiling just a little, and by the time he reached the front door, he was whistling tunelessly. I heard Dad's car start a moment later.

Mom and I exchanged grins.

When Dad came down, I asked him when he'd be available to take Rowan and me shopping for things for the tree house. Mom smiled encouragingly at him while she gathered up her stuff, kissed both of us briefly, and left.

Dad, peering suspiciously into the refrigerator as if he'd never seen the contents before, said, "You mean in the evening at those rare times when *I* get to use a car?" he asked. "I don't care when we go. Anytime except tonight, because I don't want to miss that program about cannibals on PBS."

"Grady gets off early today," I said. "We could go this afternoon while he's mowing the lawn." Then I explained that he would have to meet Rowan's parents first, before she could go anywhere with us.

"They're being cautious," he said as he pulled out a package of sliced cheese and jars of mustard and mayonnaise. "These days you have to be."

"Are you making a cheese sandwich for breakfast?" I asked when I saw what he was doing. "Didn't Mom tell you to eat cereal in the morning?"

"Your mother left for the hospital," he said, smirking. "Okay, I'll walk around and meet Rowan's parents this morning, if anyone's home. If nobody's there, I'll try again after dinner. I suppose this shopping trip is going to cost me money?"

"A little bit, but I haven't asked for anything for my room." I hurried through breakfast and went upstairs to get my decorating magazines. As soon as I saw Rowan, I'd ask her opinion about the ideas I had.

Dad dawdled getting ready for the big trip around the block. Just about the time I was ready to ask him if he'd changed his mind, he said he was ready.

"You're going over there looking like that?" I asked. He was wearing ancient chinos and a skimpy, faded T-shirt.

"You sound like your mother," he said. "I look fine. I look like *me*. That's what this meeting is all about, isn't it? We're all going to be friends."

Good grief, I thought. Well, nothing could be done with him.

"Maybe I should go with you," I said. "That's a good idea. Rowan's family needs to meet me, too." I wasn't as enthusiastic as I tried to sound. Rowan's family—or at least her father—seemed formidable.

"Let's bring Daisy," he said. "And that baby picture of you that your mother keeps on her dresser, the one showing you scowling, with your diapers at half-mast, holding a baseball bat. Let them know the worst about us."

I didn't know if he was teasing or not, but I put Daisy's leash on her and we left the house. We had a low privet hedge in front and a circular driveway made of crushed white rock. The house next door had a fence and a blooming rose garden. We lived on a nice block where the trees were old and spread their branches across the street, almost touching each other.

"You're smiling," Dad said.

"I love it here," I answered.

Daisy pulled at the leash, as if she knew where we were going. We turned the corner and then turned another, and ahead of us I saw the bulky brick house where Rowan lived. It was surrounded by a tall black iron fence. The narrow gate was locked, so we tried the gate at the driveway, but it was locked, too. "I guess no one is home," I said.

"Probably not. But maybe there's a bell to ring," Dad said as he poked through the ivy that nearly covered the fence and part of both gates. Ivy on the fence but not on the house. Ugly, I thought.

I couldn't take my gaze off the front of the house. The blinds were pulled and the place looked vacant. The lawn was very short. There were no flowers anywhere, just a narrow path that ran to the front door and a driveway that disappeared around the corner of the house.

"How do they get packages if nobody can get in?" Dad asked, sounding puzzled.

"Maybe they're thrown over the fence," I said. "This is strange. Rowan didn't say that they kept their gates locked." Actually, she hadn't said anything about her family. I remembered the silence that followed when I told her about mine.

"I should have phoned first," Dad said. "But that's a little cold. A nice face-to-face meeting is the way things should start out."

Rowan's father is probably stuffy and wears a suit every day, I thought, looking at my dad, absent-minded and affable, and dressed like—Dad. I linked my arm through his and said, "I like you a whole lot."

"I'm broke," he said. "But I like you a whole lot, too."

We didn't talk much on the way home. I wondered what he thought about the Tucker house. It wasn't the sort of place that made you feel welcome at first sight, like our new house. Poor Rowan.

Grady came home early in the afternoon, and when he opened the kitchen door, he said, "Come out to the car and see what I've got."

I was putting Mom's best crystal glasses away on a high shelf and didn't want to climb down off the chair for nothing. "What have you got?"

"A surprise," he said.

"I hate your surprises," I told him frankly. Grady's surprises usually involved something messy or loud, or sticky stuff that removed the fillings in our teeth and gummed up our braces.

"You'll love this one. Actually, it's more than one."

Sighing, I got off the chair. "You'd better be telling the truth."

Daisy shot out the door behind me as if she knew what was coming, and she was the first one to reach the car, wriggling all over the way she did when our relatives came for holiday meals.

"What's wrong with her?" I asked.

"I bet she already knows what's inside." Grady opened the door and took out a cardboard box. Immediately, something inside began squealing.

"We found them in the ditch in front of the place where we're working," Grady said. He put the box down and opened it. Two small black puppies looked up at him, trembling and crying. "We tried to feed them but they wouldn't eat."

I knelt beside the box and picked them up. Both of them fit in my cupped hands. They were soft and silky, and they had that smell that all puppies have. "Maybe they're too little to eat by themselves," I said. "Gosh, I bet they are. Look at them! They're so scared." I'd read a lot about dogs, and sometimes I even thought about being a veterinarian. I figured I'd explain that to Mom one day when she was in an especially good mood, since she was already fantasizing that I'd be an internist like her someday.

Daisy nosed the puppies gently and they stopped crying. I put the puppies on the grass and they immediately struggled toward her. Daisy licked their heads, but they weren't inter-ested in kisses. They thought she might be a substitute Mama.

"They *were* still nursing!" I cried, angry. "Didn't you see the mother? What did you think you were doing, Grady!"

"There was no mother," Grady said. He was beginning to look worried. "We searched all over the place. We even asked at the houses across the street. Somebody dumped them off during the night, I guess."

"And left them to die," I said. "Well, we have to do some-thing right away. I'll get Dad."

I ran upstairs to the spare bedroom Dad was using as a li-brary and told him. He hurried down, took a look at the ba-bies on the grass, and said, "We'll take them to the vet right now."

Dr. Joseph had been Daisy's veterinarian since Dad first brought her home, and we trusted her. The summer before I'd helped out cleaning cages for her. She spent a few minutes looking over the puppies, and then told us that I was right. They were too young to be weaned.

"You're taking on a big job," she said. "They're hungry, and to keep them going, you'll have to feed them as often as their mother would for at least another week."

"I can do it!" I said.

Dad groaned. "You mean we all will. I don't know if I'm up to night feedings, Emily. Are you sure you want to try?"

"What else can we do?" I asked. I looked to Dr. Joseph for support.

"That's all you can do," she said. "Unless you can find a shelter that will take them in. Otherwise . . ."

She didn't need to finish the sentence. Dad said, "We'll take them, at least until they're old enough to go to permanent homes. Tell us what to do."

We went home half an hour later with the puppies and a bag of supplies. Dr. Joseph's assistant had fed both the puppies with nursing bottles before we left, and they slept all the way home in my lap.

"Maybe we could keep them," I said.

"Maybe not," Dad said.

I wasn't worried. I knew him.

When we got home, we found the back lawn half-mowed and Grady in the kitchen, eating. As usual. He had changed clothes and his hair looked wet.

"The puppies—" I began.

"The guy who lives behind us is crazy!" Grady said angrily. He scared the puppies awake.

"What happened?" Dad asked as he put the puppy supplies down on the counter.

"I was mowing along the back fence when this jerk comes out and—he must have been standing on a ladder or a chair or something—he leans over the fence and waves at me until I shut the mower off. He tells me I'm making too much noise and he wants me to quit."

I sat down and snuggled the puppies against my chest. "Are you talking about Mr. Tucker, Rowan's dad?" I asked. I felt as if my stomach was going to drop to my shoes. I didn't want trouble between our families!

"We didn't exchange names," Grady said bitterly. He took a big gulp of milk before he went on. "I told him I had to mow the lawn this afternoon and he told me I'd better not try it. So I started the mower again. I mean, who is he to tell me not to mow our lawn?" All of a sudden Grady was sounding as if he'd rather mow the lawn than anything else.

Dad nodded. "And then? Did he bother you again?"

"Yeah!" Grady almost shouted. "He came right back at me again, yelling and waving his arms, yapping about having paperwork to do and I was bothering him."

Dad sighed. "So what happened next?"

"He turned his hose on me."

"What?" Dad exclaimed.

I stared at Grady. "Mr. Tucker turned his hose on you?" The first thought I had was that nobody should treat my brother like that! My second thought was that Rowan would probably never come to the tree house again.

"Yes, he turned the hose on me!" Grady said.

"What's going on over there?" Dad said, almost to himself. "I'd better call this Tucker on the phone."

But the Tuckers' number wasn't in the telephone book. While Dad called Information, I fidgeted, wondering what would happen to my beginning friendship with Rowan. Would she come to get the Queen's Beasts and never speak to me again? But what had Grady done that was so wrong? Mowing the lawn in the afternoon isn't as bad as mowing it early on a weekend morning.

Dad hung up in disgust. "Their number is unlisted. I'll go over to the house again. If he's still there, I'll root him out and we'll find out what's going on."

"Can I come?" Grady asked. He looked a little too eager.

"No, stay here and finish the lawn," Dad said.

After he left, looking stern, I told Grady I was going out to the back fence. Maybe I could hear something. Grady came along, and he stood on the box so he could look over the fence while I leaned against it, cradling the puppies, who had fallen asleep again.

After a few minutes, we heard Dad calling, "Tucker! Are you home? Tucker! Tucker!"

Well, the whole neighborhood ought to love this, I thought. We've hardly moved in and everybody knows how loudly the Shepherds can yell.

After that, we only heard what sounded like a door slamming somewhere inside the Tucker house.

Dad came home, angry now. "I know he's home," he complained. "I saw one of the blinds move. What's wrong with him?"

"He's crazy," Grady said. "I told you that."

Dad shook his head. "Well, go out and finish the lawn. If you have any more trouble, I'll handle it from this side of the fence."

While I was busy fixing a better box for the puppies and lining it with towels, Daisy supervised with great interest and kept trying to get in the box, too. Dad stood on the back deck, watching Grady. I could tell from the glimpses I had of his face that if Mr. Tucker dared to pop up over the fence again, he would be sorry he hadn't come out earlier when Dad called him. Nothing more happened. But Rowan didn't come to the tree house that afternoon, either.

I had made plans to show her the puppies, even if I had to take them out to the tree house to do it. I had wanted to share with her my decorating plans and find out what she thought. We could have had a good time.

Mom came home, exclaimed over the puppies, who were awake and peering out of their box, and the four of us started preparing dinner together. While Grady and Dad set the table, they took turns telling Mom about horrible Mr. Tucker, whom I was prepared to hate by that time. Mom kept saying, "Hmm," as she fixed stir-fry. "Hmm," and "For heaven's sake."

"So what do you think?" I asked when Dad and Grady were through talking. "Can Rowan still come over to the tree house?"

"Of course she can," Mom said. "It sounds to me as if she could use a little normal family life."

"But she can't ever come in this house, you know," I said. "And now we'll never get permission from her parents."

"That won't stop all of us from going out to the tree house to meet her," Mom said. "All of us, including Grady."

"Aw, jeez," Grady said. "As if."

"The steps aren't too steep for you," Mom said. "You can make it. It would set her mind to rest that we aren't monsters."

After dinner, I fed the puppies while Grady watched so that he could learn, too, and when they fell asleep again, I went outside to the tree house. I hoped that perhaps Rowan would see me there and come over, that everything would be all right. But she didn't come, so I spent my time there looking more closely at the Queen's Beasts, wondering why she had carved each one, and wondering why they were all smiling. What did Rowan think about while she was carving them?

They didn't really look finished. The rough edges should be sanded off, I thought. Maybe she would like me to help.

No, she would be offended. Maybe she wanted the Beasts to be rough. Artists knew how their work should look. I stroked the bear's back and imagined that she smiled a little more.

"What are you so happy about?" I whispered to her. "Tell me."

But her happiness would stay a secret for a while.

The wind turned cold and I went inside to watch Dad's cannibal program with him. Mom sat on the floor and fed the puppies while she crooned to them. She had named them Hope and Patience. Daisy watched approvingly.

I needed hope and patience, too, for what would be coming after school started in September and I would be meeting all those new people at once. Did I even know how to make friends anymore?

I fed the puppies again at midnight, tucked them back into their box, and fell into bed, exhausted. Then, in Middle Dark, I started awake for some reason and turned on my bedside lamp. I hadn't heard a sound—not really—but Daisy was sitting up in the middle of my old yellow bedspread and staring at the window as if she had. She didn't bark, though. She seemed to be listening hard. Perhaps she was anticipating what had disturbed her the last two nights. Now that I was awake, I certainly was.

I reached out to touch her and she licked my hand quickly, then settled down again with a tired little sigh.

I turned out the light and tried to make myself comfortable. Would Rowan ever come to the tree house again? Surely her father told Rowan and her mother about his quarrel with my brother. But he would have found a way to blame Grady, of course. People like him always did. Was Rowan angry with me, now?

I didn't have a friend here in our new neighborhood. I'd ended up with no friends before and I'd been miserable, but I'd hoped that things would be different here. I'd have a new start in a new school, with my new face. There wouldn't be anyone around to call me "Scarface" or "Ugly."

Why do kids tease each other? It never made sense to me and I never took part in it when someone else was the victim. When I became the goat, I couldn't believe it was happening. Some of the same kids I'd defended before were as quick to turn on me as I had been to help them.

"Their behavior is very primitive," Mom had told me when I complained to her. "People should be brought up to be kind. You were—and they were not."

She and Dad had gone to my school to complain more than once, but nothing changed. Finally I stopped telling them about what went on during the day. I learned to stay by myself and try not to care.

—

I hadn't even told them when my best friend refused to be my partner on a field trip, and the teacher was my partner instead. I knew that Kathy didn't want to be seen with me because people turned around to stare at me. If Mom and Dad had noticed that Kathy never came to our house any longer, they were kind enough not to mention it.

I turned over in bed, miserable. I had liked Rowan. And I needed a friend, too, a little bit, anyway. I would have liked taking the bus to school with her. I might even have liked meeting the girls she called her best friends, too. Trouble between our families could put an end to my hopes. But Grady had been absolutely right and Mr. Tucker had been absolutely wrong.

Families.

Chapter 4

When I woke up the next morning, Daisy was in the box with the puppies, and she looked guilty. I bent to pat her and reassure her. She might never have had puppies of her own, but she loved Hope and Patience. "You have a stepfamily," I told her. "You fit right in here."

Hope and Patience woke up and squealed, so I carried them downstairs to feed them before I ate breakfast. Mom and Grady left, and while Dad put breakfast dishes in the dishwasher, I asked the question that had been nagging me for half an hour.

"Are you *sure* it's still all right if Rowan comes over here again?"

Dad straightened up. "Of course."

"It might be embarrassing, since her dad and Grady don't get along." I was hoping he'd offer a bit of advice. His advice was different from Mom's, who was inclined to be rather brisk and practical. Dad meandered all over the place, but eventually he came up with something that was both usable and soothing. Maybe that came from teaching history, which he said was a record of human mistakes, bungled efforts to fix those mistakes, and the persistent hope that we could live them down.

"As I recall, you can't stand C.J.'s sister, but Grady and C.J. stayed friends," Dad said.

"A sister isn't the same thing as a dad," I protested. "I don't like C.J., either, and Dilly makes me sick, but they can't give anybody orders. Rowan's dad could refuse to let her come to the tree house." Even as I said it, I wondered if he knew she did.

Dad had come to the same conclusion. "Maybe she hasn't told him. It's not as if something bad will happen to her when she's on our property, but I wouldn't like it if you were sneaking off to spend time with a stranger. You understand that, I'm sure."

I studied my bare feet while I thought. "I understand, but . . ."

"But she's your new friend, and starting a strange school all alone might not be fun," he said. He put a cup of water in the microwave and started it. "And neither is having a new ex-friend who won't speak to you any longer, right?"

I swallowed hard. I knew everything there was to know about ex-friends. Cindy, who had thrown the Frisbee I couldn't catch, had been a good friend, and the first one to desert me after she saw my scarred face. "It hurts me to look at you," she had said. It also had hurt her to be seen with me, and it wasn't long before we never went anywhere together. Not that I'd wanted to be seen in public. Not that I'd missed going places. Not that I'd cared.

Oh, I had cared! But that was over now.

"Rowan doesn't know about my face," I said. "So she wouldn't be able to tell anybody at school about me." I tried to sound hopeful.

But even as I said it, I felt terrible. I liked Rowan, and for more reasons than just having somebody to hang around with at a new school.

"We don't know how this is going to sort itself out yet," Dad said. He took the instant coffee out of the refrigerator and didn't look at me. "Grady and Tucker quarreled, but time can take care of that. I'll cut the lawn next time, and if there's a problem, I'll handle it. Tucker isn't likely to start something petty with an adult."

"Grady——" I began.

"Has never handled anything controversial very well," Dad said, grinning. The microwave beeped and Dad took out the cup of hot water. "Don't make any hasty decisions about this. Don't even form an opinion about the way things can work out. Just wait. Rest easy and wait."

He made it sound so positive and simple.

The puppies were sleeping with Daisy in the box, so I ran upstairs to shower. When I opened the door, I saw that Grady had written "Half the towel rods and shelves are mine!" on the mirror with a green felt marker. One of my towels—peach colored to keep them separate from his gray ones—had been dumped on the floor and my hair dryer had been shoved onto the shelf where I kept my skin care stuff, knocking over half the bottles. Jerk! He didn't need half of the space!

Since he had been stupid enough to leave the marker on the counter, I took it back to his room and wrote "jug ears" on the mirror inside his closet door. Bedrooms were off limits without permission in our house, but he had asked for it. And he was supposed to be ready for college?

While I was dressing in my bedroom, I glanced at my face in the mirror. Sometimes I could hardly find the place where my scar had been. Mom and Dad would have been upset if they had known that I viewed the move as an escape. No one in our family ran away from things.

I stepped back from the mirror and looked again. I was fine. I really was.

But I left the room with my stack of magazines and didn't look back. Every mirror I'd seen since the accident caused me to remember all sorts of things that were better off forgotten.

Dad spent hours puttering in the bedroom he called his "library," and I played with the puppies, changed the towels in their box, fed them, and rocked them to sleep in my lap while I sat on the deck and looked at the tree house.

What color should I paint the interior walls? Mom had suggested a light cream color, so that the small room would seem larger. But I had seen a picture in one of the decorating magazines of a small room painted red, with a gold flowered border around the ceiling. Would that be a good idea? I really wanted Rowan's advice. But maybe I would live without it.

After lunch, I unpacked my own books and put them away in my bookcase, and then I took the puppies outside for a walk around the backyard. They loved the adventure, even though they had to struggle through the grass and over every pebble. When they were tired, I moved their box out to the tree house, boosted Daisy inside, and climbed in with my magazines. The puppies fell asleep instantly, curled into a soft black ball. Daisy, tired of puppy-sitting, jumped up on the bench where Rowan usually sat and stretched out for a nap.

I turned pages and listened to the breeze in the maple tree, stirring the green and silver leaves and whispering around the roof of my small refuge. One of the puppies yelped softly in her sleep and I bent to pat her carefully and reassure her.

"Emily?" Rowan climbed the steps, smiling. Daisy jumped down to greet her and the puppies woke crying and scratched the sides of the box with their tiny toenails. Rowan knelt beside the box and exclaimed over Hope and Patience.

"Where did you get them?" she asked. "Are they yours?"

"My brother found them. They weren't weaned, so we're taking turns feeding them."

Rowan's eyes looked shocked behind her glasses. "Your brother *found* them? Were they lost?"

"They'd been dumped, left in a box by the side of a road. Mom named them Hope and Patience. This one is Hope." I picked up the smaller puppy, and handed her to Rowan. "Isn't she cute? She's got one white toe, see?"

Rowan smiled over the puppy, admiring her white toe and her small ears. "Are you going to keep them?"

"I hope so. Dad says we'll find homes for them, but I bet he won't want to when the time comes. If he tries, I'll talk him out of it."

Rowan sat with Hope in her lap until she fell asleep and then she put her back in the box. "She's so sweet," Rowan said. "I wish I could have a dog, but . . ."

"But what?"

She glanced over her shoulder, through the window, to where her house scowled across the fence at ours. "There's hardly ever anyone home in the daytime, except for me during school vacation. Well, Dad works there sometimes, but he doesn't like dogs or cats. Or any kind of pets."

Did she know that her father didn't like Grady, either? Had she been home when her father was yelling at Grady? There was no way I could ask—and I was afraid of the answers. Maybe this was something we'd never *need* to talk about. Maybe everything could stay just the way it was now, peaceful and positive, with no bad news.

Rowan saw the stack of magazines and asked me if we were still redecorating the house.

"Mom says we'll do something with the living and dining rooms someday," I said. "But I like them just like they are. Some of the pictures in the magazines are really nice, sort of Victorian, and Mom says that style would fit our house."

"It would fit the tree house, too," Rowan said.

"That's what I was thinking. Mom said I could paint and get a rug and some cushions for the benches. Dad's taking me shopping tonight. Do you want to come with us?" I didn't want to bring up our effort to invite her earlier.

I could tell from her face that she wanted to go, but she shook her head. "I can't tonight."

"We could go tomorrow," I said, knowing that I was pushing her.

She looked trapped, and I was sorry immediately. "It's because your family doesn't know mine, right?" I asked. I *hoped* that was the reason. I didn't want Grady's quarrel with Mr. Tucker to be the cause. Or Dad's calling her father's loud enough to be heard on the moon.

Actually, I thought defensively, Mr. Tucker had been the one who had quarreled with Grady. Mr. Tucker had started it. And he had been rude, not coming to the door when Dad was outside.

Rowan picked up a magazine and began turning pages. "My parents worry about strangers," she said. "It's silly, really. I'm old enough to take care of myself, but Dad doesn't like Mom and me to . . ." I could see that she had caught herself on the verge of telling something she would regret. She blinked nervously and I wondered if she was even seeing what was on the pages.

I needed to change the subject. I handed her another magazine and said, "See if you find something that looks like it could be the inside of a tree house."

She laughed at that. "I don't think the people who put together decorating magazines ever think about tree houses." But she took the magazine and paged through it. I looked through mine, too, and there was a wonderful kind of silence in the tree house, the kind that doesn't make anyone feel uncomfortable and doesn't need to be interrupted with small talk.

After a while, Rowan held up a magazine and said, "Look."

I'd seen the picture of the window alcove before. The long, narrow cushion was just what I wanted for the benches. "I hope I can find something like that tonight," I said. "Dad's not a happy shopper, and neither is my mom."

"My mom likes to shop," Rowan said as she turned another

page in the magazine. "She doesn't go very often, but she really likes it."

"Your mom works?" I asked. Here was a chance to learn something about Rowan's family.

Rowan nodded, said, "Um hm," and turned another page.

"What does she do?" I asked.

"She works for a software company," she said. She didn't look up, but turned the magazine sideways so that she could see a picture from a different angle.

"Does she like it?"

Rowan looked up then and blinked while she thought. "I guess so."

"Where does your dad work?" I asked.

I felt the wave of distress that washed over her.

She turned another page. "He's an engineering consultant. He travels around the country a lot." She let her voice drop the way people do when they don't want to say any more.

So Mr. Tucker traveled a lot. Good. That meant that Rowan could do what she wanted when he was out of town. I would.

Rowan put down the magazines and pulled out the same sharp knife she had used before on the unicorn. "I'm glad I have a chance to work on this today," she said as she took it off the shelf. "I had an idea about carving a collar of flowers on her. Would you like that?"

"I'll like whatever you do," I said. "Are your Beasts like the ones in England?"

"Oh, no," she said, concentrating on her work. A thin scroll of wood curled out from under the knife. "Most of the real Queen's Beasts are mythical creatures. Even the ones that could be real are very stylized. My Beasts are all real, except for the unicorn I'm making for you, and I've tried to make them look as natural as possible. I thought that you'd like a mythical beast best, though."

"Why?" It was a strange comment and I wanted to know why she thought I would like a mythical beast better than a real one.

"Real animals sometimes have very sad lives," she said without looking up. "You don't seem like someone who ever wants to be sad."

I laughed a little, surprised. "Who would *want* to be sad?" I asked.

"Some people do," she said quietly.

I wondered if she meant one or the other of her parents. Or herself. But who would *want* to be sad? There was a good question to ask Dad. But not Mom. I could already hear what she would say. "They want to be sad because there is a payoff somewhere," Mom would say. She had told me once that most negative behavior came because the person with that behavior had figured out a way to get something with it, and that person wouldn't give it up willingly.

"So you carve real animals most of the time because . . ." I waited for her to fill in the rest of the sentence.

"Sometimes they need to be remembered in a special way," she said. "So I remember them here." She put down the unicorn and the knife and picked up a small carved cat. "See? This is Libby, my grandmother's cat."

"The one in England?"

Rowan nodded. "She's wonderful. She slept on the foot of my bed when I was staying with them. I like having pets in the house. Grandmother had framed snapshots of every pet my mother had when she was growing up there. They were on the dresser in the bedroom Mom and I shared."

So I had learned something new. Her mother had been born in England and she liked pets.

"You want to remember Libby in a special way because you had so much fun with her," I said. "That's nice."

But the expression on Rowan's face told me that there was more to the story. However, she put the cat back on the shelf and picked up a small wooden dog. A smile spread across her face.

"This is Stubby," she said.

"Stubby!" I cried. "Do you mean the Bonners' dog?"

She looked surprised. "Did they tell you about him?"

"We found his collar," I told her. "You knew him?"

"Oh, sure. He was still alive when I first started coming here. I helped him up the steps, because he was awfully stiff. He liked being in here. I was really sorry when he died, so I carved him in wood. I know I didn't do a very good job, but I liked his company, so in a way he's still here with me."

"Like Libby," I said.

"But in a different way," Rowan said. "The carving of Libby is like . . . like a promise. Stubby is like a memory that doesn't ever go away."

"You want to see Libby again, so that's why it's a promise," I said.

Rowan put Stubby back on the shelf. "Something like that," she said. She touched the small dog's head once more and then picked up the carving of a larger dog, one that looked a little like a retriever.

"I named this dog Traveler," she said. "When I hold him, I think of him traveling on soft dirt roads through beautiful farmland, with a good place to sleep every night and plenty of friends and all he can eat. The weather is never too hot or too cold, and it never rains, and there are no cars or cruel people. And maybe somebody who is kind and gentle walks with him once in a while, if he wants that. But only if he wants it, because in his world, in this place with fields and soft roads, he gets to create everything."

I liked her voice. When she talked about her Beasts, she sounded like the storyteller who had come to the hospital in the afternoons and sat in the atrium, telling stories to the kids who were patients.

"And Traveler was a real dog?" I asked.

She nodded. "We found him dead in a trap. He had a collar, and Mom called the phone number on it and told the people what had happened to their dog. They came and got him. Traveler doesn't have to wear a collar now, because he always knows where he is."

I had a lump in my throat and my eyes stung. "I always feel so bad when animals die," I said.

"I like to think of them afterward as being in a safe place at last, with other animals who are really glad to see them. Always glad." She was looking down again when she said that so it was hard to see her face, but I wondered if she was almost ready to cry. But when she looked up, she was smiling and her green eyes sparkled behind her thick glasses. *"Always glad,"* she repeated firmly.

That was a wonderful thought, and I was about to tell her so when she said, "I guess I'd better go home. I've got some things I have to do."

"But you've only been here a little while," I protested.

She stood up, put her knife in her pocket, and returned the unfinished unicorn to the shelf. "I really have to go. Tomorrow I'll bring over some magazines I've saved. They're all about Victorian things. Maybe you'll get some ideas, if you don't find what you want tonight."

She bent over the puppies and patted them, then left. I watched her through the window as she made her way through the trees and finally climbed up on the box and boosted herself over the fence. I knew no one was home watching her. I had figured out many things about her, and one was that she would never come to the tree house on the days her father was working at home.

Maybe he'll go out of town and stay for the rest of the summer, I thought. She might have wished that, too.

After dinner, Dad took me shopping at the mall, and neither of us had a very good time. I found a rug I wanted, but Dad said he wasn't going to pay as much money for a small rug as he paid for a new kitchen, so I'd better scale down my expectations.

"I think I'd rather go shopping with Mom," I told him bluntly.

"She hates shopping, remember?" he said. "If you go with her, you'll only end up in a bookstore where she'll buy you another stack of science books. Stick with me, kid, and we'll furnish your tree house."

"Dad!" I said. "Don't call me 'kid'—and I wanted that rug!"

"You don't need a silk rug handmade by elves," he said. He pointed at the bargain import store. "Let's go there. They'll have rugs."

"I want a rug that looks Victorian," I said firmly. "And I want soft squishy cushions with flowers."

Dad smacked his hand on his forehead. "Of course you do," he said. "I'm sure soft and squishy doesn't come cheap, either. I think . . ."

I did not hear the rest of what he said because I had just seen someone I knew, and the shock left me deaf. Dilly Sanderson, C.J.'s mean sister, was pushing her way through the crowd going into the video store. I had known her in my old school, and she had been one of my tormentors. "Scarface!" "Ugly!" The words still rang in my mind.

I turned my back and began walking toward the mall exit. "Come on, Dad," I said over my shoulder. "Let's talk to Mom about this."

"Well, all right," Dad said, puzzled. I did not look back to see if he was following me, but hurried toward the bank of glass doors leading out to the parking lot. Dilly must not see me.

He caught up with me at the car. I kept my face turned toward the highway beyond the parking lot, as if something there fascinated me. "What's wrong?" he asked. "You ran out of there as if you'd seen a ghost."

"It's so crowded in the mall tonight," I said. "Maybe we should come back right after dinner next week sometime." At that moment, I did not care if I ever got a rug for the tree house. All I could think of was Dilly. I had hoped I would never see her again, or anyone else from my old school. I did not want to be reminded of the miserable times I had endured there after my accident. I wanted to forget the whispers—and then the shouts. "Hey, Ugly, what happened to you?"

Hey, Ugly, what had happened to *me?*

After we got in the car, I touched my face once, carefully, for reassurance. I lived in a different house now, and I would be going to a different school, and sad Emily had been left behind. I was starting all over with new people who did not know that I had ever been ugly.

Chapter 5

Hope and Patience slept through the next night, except for a brief period when Daisy barked during Middle Dark. The rest of us were becoming accustomed to her nighttime alarms and no one got out of bed to see what was going on. I even wondered if she hadn't heard anything at all, but had only been expecting something and decided to get in the first word. She settled down after a few sharp yaps and a drawn out, soft growl, but the puppies had awakened, so I had to turn on the bedside lamp and pat them until they fell back to sleep.

"You shouldn't wake up the babies," I told Daisy. Her look told me that she was only doing her duty. But I lay awake for a while, wondering if everything was all right at Rowan's house.

That afternoon, Rowan showed up in the tree house with six magazines filled with photos of Victorian rooms and furnishings. She was wearing jeans that fit her for once, and a bright pink T-shirt, and her hair was clipped to one side neatly. Some of the magazine pages had red flags, and she held up one photograph after another, saying, "Look at this, Emily!" and "You'll love this."

I agreed with her opinion about every page. Yes, we did need light walls in the tree house, and we needed to hang pictures to make the place seem even friendlier.

"I've got some pressed wildflowers in frames, like the ones in this photograph," Rowan said. "Would you like to see them? I made them myself, and they might look nice in here."

I studied the page. There was a table under them with an elaborate vase filled with roses. "Yes," I told her, pleased. "Bring the wildflowers. And we could use a vase of silk flowers in here so we'd have something cheerful in winter. But there isn't room for a table."

"There's room for the vase in the corner, on the floor," Rowan said.

We smiled at each other, satisfied. What one of us didn't think of, the other one did. By the time we were through, the tree house would belong in a magazine.

When it was time for the puppies' afternoon feeding, I let Rowan give it to them. "Hope's my favorite," she said. "She's the smallest and she needs the most attention, doesn't she?"

"Yes. Daisy licks her the most, so she agrees with us."

"I wish . . ." Rowan began, but she did not finish the sentence. That was all right. I knew what she was going to say. She wanted to keep Hope herself.

After Hope went to sleep, Rowan began working on the unicorn again. "Do you believe that there ever were unicorns?" she asked. Her head was bent over the carving and I couldn't read her expression.

"Why not?" I said. "How can we know about every animal

that ever existed? In science class, we learned that new fossils are discovered all the time."

"I wonder if all the Queen's Beasts in England ever existed?" she said. "Do you suppose they did and that's how come people believed in them a long time ago?"

"I like that idea!" I said. "It sounds like a fantasy novel, where people and mythical beasts lived in the same places."

I took Rowan's whale down from the shelf and examined it closely. Its wise and friendly expression made me smile. "Tell me about the whale," I said, eager to hear another of her stories. "Did you actually see it somewhere?"

She shook her head and looked down. She was silent for a moment, and then she said, "I read in the news that she was killed. She was only a baby, but now she can swim forever between Mexico where the water is warm and the Arctic where it's cold, just the way all the other gray whales choose to do. No one can ever hurt her again. No one will ever frighten her again, either. She'll be with her mother forever and she'll be happy forever, too."

It was hard not to cry. But I loved the idea that Rowan's carving could give the whale another life. While she spoke about it, I had almost seen the pretty creature swimming, dappled by the sunlight shining through the water or gleaming in moonlight, but always safe. Forever safe.

Listening to Rowan fed my imagination. My favorite subject in school was always science, but I'd had an art class. Maybe I'd try to draw again. I'd never been very good, but when Rowan talked, I could see things that I had never dreamed of before, and I wanted to save these visions somehow.

She was different from anyone I'd ever known. The friends I'd once had couldn't tell stories, and now that I thought about it, they hadn't been interested in much except their own lives. But then, I had been like that, too. If I'd ever deliberately created a picture in my mind before, it had been of me winning in a soccer game or doing more laps in a pool than anyone else.

I put the whale back and picked up the elephant. "What about the elephant?" I asked.

Rowan looked up at me then, smiling. "Her name is Wide Awake. A long time ago the children in Seattle bought her with pennies they had saved. She lived at the zoo for the rest of her life. My fourth grade teacher told us about her and I liked the story, but I wondered if she missed the place where she was born. Now that I've carved her, she can live forever in her real home in Asia, deep in a forest where no one can find her except her friends." She reached for the elephant, rubbed her head, and then returned her to me. "In India," she said, "they have a god named Lord Ganesha, and he's called the Remover of Obstacles. Don't you like that idea?"

I could see an elephant moving silently through a deep tropical forest, followed by the other elephants in her herd. But I could see a ferocious elephant pushing down a wall, too.

"I could use a Remover of Obstacles," I said, thinking suddenly of C.J. Grady would be so much better off without him. What my brother needed was a best friend with ideas like Rowan's. Somebody who was imaginative. Somebody who wasn't stuck on himself.

I put the elephant back and then I patted the small heads

of Libby and Stubby. Rowan's magic had made me believe that they could actually feel it.

"I keep forgetting to ask my mom for the snapshots she took of the Queen's Beasts," I said

"I imagine she's got too much to do right now," Rowan said placidly.

"You'd like her," I said. "And my dad, too."

"I'm sure I would," she said. She didn't say anything about her parents, though, and she fell into a silence that didn't seem to bother her at all.

I turned magazine pages, and Rowan worked on the unicorn. Hope whimpered a little in her sleep, and her paws twitched as if she were running. Daisy leaned into the box and licked Hope's face until she settled down. Then, without warning, Daisy stood up and looked out the door, wagging her stub of a tail.

Mom appeared at the top of the steps. "Hi, everybody," she said. "May I come in?"

She didn't wait for permission, but came in and sat down on the bench next to me. I introduced Mom and Rowan, but I saw Rowan stiffen.

"How come you're home so early?" I asked Mom quickly, to prevent one of those silences that could be so awful.

"I gave myself the afternoon off," Mom said brightly.

I knew that she saw how anxious Rowan was. She didn't give Rowan a chance to stay miserable for long, though. "I'm so glad to finally meet you, Rowan," she said, and she leaned forward with her elbows on her knees. "Have the two of you decided how the place should be decorated?"

"I'm going to paint the inside a light color," I said. "Rowan's bringing framed wildflowers to hang on the walls."

"My mother pressed wildflowers," Mom said, smiling. "I'd forgotten how pretty they were. When will you bring them over, Rowan?"

I had a hunch that Rowan had not planned to say a single word, but Mom had asked a question so she had to answer.

She looked down at the unicorn she still held and said, "Whenever Emily wants them."

Mom noticed the Queen's Beasts then, and said, "These are what you were talking about, Emily! They're wonderful." She picked up the elephant and smiled into its smiling face. "Aww, I love this."

"It's Wide Awake," I said.

"I've heard of her," Mom said. "Oh, look, Emily. All the animals are smiling. Had you noticed that?"

"Only the first time I saw them, Mom," I said. I wanted to tell her that Rowan had a story for each one, too, but I was sure that Rowan should be the one to talk about that, and if she didn't want to, then that would be all right, too.

Mom asked to see the unicorn and praised Rowan for it. "I've always loved unicorns," she said. "Once I had a small silver one I wore on a chain, but I lost it somehow, and I always felt as if I'd lost a friend."

My first impulse was to tell Mom that she could have my Beast as soon as Rowan finished it, but luckily I thought before I said it. If Mom wanted another unicorn, I'd find her one for her next birthday.

I showed Mom the rest of Rowan's magazines instead, and

the three of us talked about decorating the tree house. Or rather, Mom and I talked. Rowan listened and glanced up at Mom many times, as if she were studying her closely. Once I saw her begin to smile, then stop, as if she didn't want to appear to be having too good a time.

As if maybe having a good time wasn't quite safe.

Mom liked all our ideas, which was good, since she and Dad would be paying for them. I was certain that Mom had come home deliberately, hoping to meet Rowan, because as time passed, many of her comments were directed at Rowan, not me.

But she wasn't very successful in drawing Rowan out. Rowan answered direct questions briefly and seldom looked up. She was polite and spoke in an ordinary voice, not the storyteller's voice she used so well. I wished that Mom could hear her, but I was sure I'd be making a huge mistake if I asked Rowan to explain the Beasts.

When the puppies woke, Rowan put her knife away and gathered them up in her lap.

"They're sweet, aren't they, Rowan?" Mom asked. "I don't know what we'll do with them when they're older, though. Do you know of anyone who wants a dog and would give her a good home?"

Rowan hesitated, then said, "I'll ask my friends Lorna and Carlene. They might know someone." She put Hope and Patience back in their box and returned the unicorn to the shelf. "I should be going now. I'm glad I met you, Mrs. Shepherd."

"Come and have dinner with us sometime," Mom said.

But Rowan didn't respond except to say, "Good-bye," as she hurried down the steps. I watched through the window while she almost ran to the fence.

"Did I scare her off?" Mom asked. "Oh, dear. She shot out of here like a frightened rabbit."

"I think she's really shy. You'd have to meet her parents before she could come over for dinner, and even then . . . well, after Grady and her father got into that argument, I'm not sure her parents would let her go inside our house."

"You said Grady's name as if you held him responsible for what happened," Mom said.

I shrugged. "No, I know that he wasn't. I just wish it hadn't happened."

Mom sighed. "So do I, but we can't run our lives with wishes. You and Rowan can be friends, though, even if her father is mean-spirited."

"Sure, as long as I don't go to her house and she doesn't come to mine," I said, exasperated. What kind of friendship can endure with rules like that?

"I wonder if her parents know she comes over to the tree house," Mom said slowly.

So Dad hadn't told her.

I shrugged again. I thought the Tuckers didn't know, but I didn't want to say that. Mom had strong negative feelings about people sneaking around. I didn't want to talk about Rowan anymore, so I picked up the whining puppies and told Mom that they needed to be fed.

After dinner, I tried to persuade Dad to take me shopping, but he told me to ask Mom for a ride, because he absolutely had to search through his file cabinets for important material he was afraid he had lost when we moved. I didn't believe a word, but I let him off, and he actually whistled as he walked upstairs.

Mom hated shopping. When I wanted clothes, she let me shop alone while she waited in a coffee shop and read a book. She bought her own clothes from catalogs and the Internet or called department stores and asked clerks to pick things out for her and send them. Grady said Mom dressed as if she borrowed clothes from a color-blind environmentalist, but then he'd told me a dozen times that I spent too much time fussing over what I wore.

"What about catalogs?" Mom asked, just as I expected. "What about looking on the Internet for the things you want for the tree house?"

"I want to go to *stores*," I said. "I want to look at things and touch them and think about them."

"Good grief," Mom muttered. "Okay, I'll take you, but you'll owe me for this."

She drove us to an import store on the other side of Seattle, a place she had heard about from a patient. We found a rug that was exactly right and a big vase for artificial flowers. Mom also found a china tea set that looked a little like one we'd seen in a magazine, except that it wasn't English and it didn't cost much.

"You must have a tea set in the tree house," she said. "And

you need cloth napkins, if you're going to do this right. Paper napkins won't do." We found white ones that suited her in another part of the store.

"But we don't have a table for all this," I said. "There isn't much room in the tree house."

"The table doesn't need to be big," Mom said. "You won't sit at it, you'll just put the tea things on it."

We found exactly the right table in a store at the other end of the block. It wasn't much larger than a dinner plate—and it cost more than everything else together.

"Dad would have a fit over this," I said. "He's still grumbling about how much the bathrooms cost."

"It's for a good cause," Mom said. "Now we need to find those cushions."

We didn't find anything that looked right, though, and both of us were disappointed when we drove home. "You and Rowan will think of something," Mom said. "Let me know what you decide."

I could see the tree house as a project that would take a long time and perhaps need changing now and then as I found new ideas in magazines and stores. That was all right with me. Everything about our new home was all right with me.

The house was the kind of place that invited people in for a visit. Since our move, several of my parents' friends had come by with housewarming gifts. Grady's friends, including his girlfriend Melanie and two girls I'd never met before, had wandered all over the place when he was home, talking constantly, playing the living room stereo too loud, and emptying the refrigerator. The girls had asked a dozen questions about Hope and Patience, and the boys had told him about cars they'd seen for sale at great prices.

None of the kids I knew had come or called. Of course, I hadn't told anyone that I was moving, either, although people in my old neighborhood must have noticed. I didn't care. I was out of reach then.

Mom told Dad that our shopping trip had been successful, and he carried our purchases from the car to the house, grumbling the whole time. Only C.J. was there with Grady, and he just glanced at us as we walked through the living room where they were watching a movie, eating sandwiches, and scattering crumbs.

"Grady, C.J., both of you take your feet off the coffee table unless you want to get me a new one," Mom said automatically as we passed.

Grady groaned and C.J. snickered. But both of them got up without a word and thundered upstairs to my brother's room.

I'd never understood why Grady liked him. C.J. had a bad habit of laughing at things that weren't funny. His sneer drove me crazy. He'd been given a car for his sixteenth birthday, wrecked it a week later, and his parents had just given him another when he graduated from high school. Grady envied him for the car, at least. I couldn't imagine what else he saw in him, unless he found C.J.'s life to be exciting. Maybe, compared to Grady's, it was. C.J. went out every night, he bragged. Of course, he had barely graduated from high school, while my brother was an honor student and had won a college scholarship.

As far as I knew, the only time Grady and he had ever quarreled was when C.J. said something about my face. Grady hadn't told me what it was, but he had hit C.J. so hard that they had stopped speaking to each other for a month. Our parents never learned about that, even though I was really grateful.

But they made up again, and now C.J. was at our new home so much that I wondered if he wanted to live with us. Fat chance. Mom and Dad were not crazy about him, either.

I took Hope and Patience upstairs with me for a feeding and watched TV in my room for a while. The puppies didn't settle down this time, but wandered around my room, sniffing everything and wagging their tails. Both of them left puddles which had to be cleaned up. Daisy sniffed disdainfully at the spots in front of my dresser and then looked at me as if I should have prevented this. Obviously she did not remember when she was a puppy.

Puppies were more work than I had thought, but they were worth it. Would Dad let me keep Hope and Patience?

I had to get paper towels from the linen closet and passed Grady's room on the way. His door was ajar and I didn't mean to eavesdrop, but I heard C.J. say, ". . . and I'm sure I can fix it up so that nobody . . ." I kept walking but I wondered what C.J. was plotting that time. He seemed to spend half of his time thinking up ways to entertain himself and annoy other people.

On my way back to my room, I yawned noisily, hoping C.J. would hear me and maybe go home. Grady yelled, "Emily!" I kept going, grinning.

Mom stuck her head in through my doorway then, saw

what I was doing, and laughed. "You'd better read up on housebreaking."

"Will Dad let us keep them?" I asked. "They're so cute!"

"Honey," Mom said, protesting. "What would we do with three dogs running around here?"

"We could enjoy their company. We've got plenty of room, so the puppies could have their own bedroom."

"Ask Rowan if she's talked to her friends the next time you see her," Mom said, and she walked away quickly, as if she was afraid I would ask again to keep the puppies and she might give in that time.

So I might ask Rowan, I decided. Maybe. Or maybe I'd forget and we'd talk about other things.

I didn't see her again for several days, and I missed her. I had never hesitated to call my friends in the good old days, before the accident. If I hadn't heard from them for a day or so, I'd phone and ask them what they were doing. In those good old days, they always seemed to be glad I called.

But I couldn't call Rowan. Even if I had her phone number, I still couldn't call. Her father might not like it. I hadn't met him, but I couldn't decide if he scared me or disgusted me.

Chapter 6

On Tuesday I woke up late and heard the light patter of rain on the roof. When I let Daisy out of my room, she shot downstairs to join the puppies, who were squeaking in the kitchen. I could hear Dad talking to them and couldn't help but grin. By the time they were old enough to go to new homes, he wouldn't be able to part with them.

I gathered up clean clothes and padded barefoot to the bathroom. What a mess! Grady had splattered toothpaste all over the basin. I wished that just once Mom would make him come back home and clean up after himself. But after September, he'd be his roommate's problem. I might miss him a little, but I wouldn't miss cleaning up after him. He wasn't charming, like the puppies. I didn't mind cleaning up after them.

My mind was on them when I pulled open the shower door, so what I saw didn't register with me in the first few seconds. But then I stopped cold and held my breath. Darn Grady anyway!

He'd emptied out both of my drawers and dumped everything on the floor of the shower, along with my hair dryer, my bath towels, and the mat. On the wall, he'd written, *Stay out of my bedroom,* but not in green ink that time. He'd used the dark lipstick I'd experimented with and decided not to wear because of the color, which was awful. Why had I taken it with me when we moved?

I swiped at the lipstick with a handful of tissues. It smeared. I sprayed clouds of shower cleaner on the tile. Now the letters just drooped a little and looked as if they said, *"Slaw onn t me dedruum."*

Gritting my teeth, I opened the door to let the chemical fumes out and then I rubbed the words off with Grady's bath towel. Serves him right, I thought.

Daisy came in and watched me with interest, probably because I was muttering rather loudly.

Dad followed her. "Should I ask about this?" he inquired carefully.

"Exactly how many days before Grady moves into the dorm?" I asked as I threw Grady's towel into the corner.

Dad sighed. "Too many, from the looks of this place. Did he throw all that stuff in the shower?"

"I certainly didn't do that, Dad!" I complained. "I ought to kill him."

"Do it outside on the lawn, please," he said as he turned to leave. "I can't afford carpet cleaning right now."

The problem with brothers is that they drive you crazy, but then there's family loyalty, too. There had been times when I longed to bash Grady with a blunt instrument, but when his first girlfriend, Bibi Jacobi, broke up with him, I cried and wanted her to come down with something that was not only painful and ugly, but also terminal. Did my brother remember that? No, he was acting like a kid, and probably C.J. was urging him on. Was he going to spend the rest of his life making people mad at him because he followed C.J.'s lead?

I hated family hassles, although I had begun a few myself. But I didn't play practical jokes! Well, not too many. As far as I was concerned, practical jokes were the same as teasing, and I hated things like that. While we argued with one another sometimes, we always avoided all-out catastrophe. However, brothers needed to be straightened out.

I ate breakfast alone, sitting on the deck and thinking about the tree house, since I wasn't likely to improve my mood by thinking about my brother. Daisy and the puppies lay beside me, sniffing the air and pretending that they knew everything that went on in the neighborhood.

I had spent the day before sanding the interior walls of the tree house, getting ready to paint. Now, dressed in my oldest shorts and shirt, I carried a can of paint, a brush, and a stack of newspapers out there. The rain had stopped, the sun came out, and the yard smelled wonderful, like summer.

Before I'd begun sanding, I had taken down the Queen's Beasts and the unicorn and put them carefully in a box. I moved the box outside now and put newspapers down on the tree house floor. Dad had told me to paint the ceiling first, and it didn't take long. I knew I had paint in my hair, but I didn't care. By the time the ceiling was done, the place seemed much lighter. Painted walls would make it seem even better.

I was nearly done by lunchtime. Dad fixed us sandwiches and brought them out to the tree house.

"It looks good," he said as he handed me a paper plate. "Has your friend come by to check it out?"

"I haven't seen Rowan," I said, my mouth full. "I hope she likes it—if she comes back."

Dad didn't respond to that. He was probably thinking the same thing I was. The two families had gotten off to a bad start, thanks to Rowan's father.

As soon as Dad finished his sandwich, he went back to the house for cookies and pop. I was sitting in the middle of the small room, looking around and congratulating myself, when Rowan came up the steps, wearing striped shorts and a new white T-shirt.

"You've painted!" she exclaimed. "The place is beautiful!"

I offered her the last of my potato chips and said, "You sure look nice. You make me look like a ragbag. Your hair is great."

"It's like yours," she said. "I hope you don't mind that I copied you. I would have come over to help you paint if I'd known you were going to do it so soon."

"I could have called you if I'd had your number," I said, hoping I didn't sound as if I were twisting her arm. "Maybe we could exchange phone numbers."

She blinked and hesitated just long enough for me to feel awful. Maybe I didn't remember how to make friends any longer. Even when she said, "Yes, we should do that," I still felt bad. I did not understand her at all! Surely her father would allow her to have phone calls! Or perhaps he wouldn't want her to have calls from Grady's sister. Or perhaps she only wanted to be neighborly, which certainly isn't the same thing as being friendly.

I struggled to think up something to say and finally blurted, "Mom and I got a rug and a table."

"Great," she said. She was looking around and suddenly I remembered the Beasts.

"I put the Queen's Beasts in a box and left it outside. I didn't want to get paint on them."

She smiled then and seemed relieved. "How long will it take the paint to dry?"

"It's supposed to dry right away." I reached up and ran one finger over the paint on the ceiling. It was fine. "I should be able to put the rug in anytime."

"I can hardly wait," Rowan said. "It's going to be wonderful. It already *is* wonderful. I'll bring over the pressed flowers, next time I come."

Dad came back and climbed the steps then, saw Rowan, and said cheerfully, "Hello there!"

Rowan actually flinched. It was hard to pretend that I didn't notice. I introduced them hastily and Dad told her he would get more pop from the kitchen. "You drink mine now," he said, and he handed her his unopened can without giving her a chance to refuse. He handed her the sack of cookies next. "Share them half and half with Emily. I already had a few."

Rowan nodded speechlessly and Dad left again.

"We can't sit on the benches because they're still wet," I said. "Would you like to go up to the house and sit on the deck?"

"No, thank you," she said hastily. "I don't mind standing."

So my deck was too close to my house for comfort, I

thought. I had never known anyone as shy as Rowan. The noisy Shepherd family would probably be too much for her.

Dad returned with his pop, but he didn't come through the door. "This place is a little small. Rowan, how long have you lived in this neighborhood?"

It was a question I'd never thought to ask. My parents were better at getting people to talk than I'd ever be.

"We've been here since I started kindergarten," Rowan said. Dad and I waited for her to add something, because people usually filled in a few details if they got the chance, but she didn't say another word.

The silence bothered Dad more than it bothered her. "Do you like the schools here?" Dad asked.

Rowan nodded and passed the bag of cookies to me. "The high school building is new," she said.

There was another pause, and then Dad filled it with a hearty, "That's good."

I tried to read Dad's mind, to see if he liked Rowan, but I couldn't be sure that he did. He had the knack of being perfectly polite to someone, even though he had no interest in ever talking to that person again. He was different from Mom, who could seem as if she was in another room behind a closed door, even when someone was close enough to touch her. Sometimes I thought that she liked sick people best, after her family.

"I'll leave you two to your dessert," Dad said. "Glad to have met you, Rowan. Come over any time."

So it was all right, then. I took my first good breath since Dad had showed up. He never invited people to come over to our house unless he liked them. He had never said such a thing to C.J., for instance. C.J. came anyway. Sigh.

"Your father is nice," Rowan said suddenly. She smiled, too. Then she added, "Sorry, I meant stepfather."

"No, *father,*" I said cheerfully. "He's the only one I've ever known. My natural father was somebody my mother met during her hospital residency. He decided to start his practice in another state and he never said anything until he was packing to leave. Mom hadn't told him I was on the way yet and she made up her mind that he wasn't very good 'dad' material. So that was that." I loved telling the story, because I really believed that families were made up of the people you *wanted,* not the people you were stuck with.

Rowan stared at me. "She never told him about you? Do you know who he is?"

"Nope," I said. I shrugged and grinned at her. "I've never asked either."

"Wow," Rowan said. She shook her head and seemed to be marveling at this news. "It's okay with you?" she asked. "It's all right that your mother did that?"

"I've got a terrific dad," I said. "Don't you think so?"

Rowan glanced toward the tree house door, as if she expected Dad to pop in again. "He really is nice," she said slowly. "Your mother was brave, to start all over like that. But look who she found, a good father for you and a big brother. Does Grady's mother . . ." She stopped and flushed a little.

"Dad got custody of Grady when he was a baby. We've never seen her."

"And nobody cares?" Rowan asked. She looked almost shocked again.

I shook my head. "Why should we? We're already a real family."

After that, I was sure she'd say something about her family, but she didn't, and even though I was tempted, I didn't ask questions.

The conversation we'd had about my family made what happened later that day seem even worse.

Rowan finished the painting for me, careful not to get paint on her clothes. While she worked, she said, "I want you to meet Lorna and Carlene. Maybe I'll call them and we could all get together somewhere. You could bring the puppies."

"Sure," I said, even though I didn't like the idea of someone wanting to adopt Hope or Patience. "When?"

Rowan stopped painting and thought for a moment, then said, "Tomorrow? My dad . . ." She paused and then said, "We could meet at the pond in the park on Andrews Street around one o'clock. It's a nice place."

"I've seen it. I'd like that." Even as I said it, I wondered if I wanted to meet her friends. This was a big step to take, and I hadn't had time to think about it. Meeting Rowan when I did had been a surprise, but it turned out all right. Meeting even more people when I hadn't had a chance to plan for it first made my stomach knot.

After Rowan left, I went in the house to clean up. Dad was puttering around upstairs in his library and I stood in the doorway watching him for a moment.

"Everything okay?" he asked when he saw me.

"Rowan asked me to meet a couple of her friends tomorrow in that little park down the hill."

He looked up from a ragged old map and said, "Good. You'll know lots of people before you start school. You'll have somebody to eat lunch with. That bothered me a lot when I was new in a school."

"She wants me to bring the puppies with me to the park."

Dad pushed up his glasses, frowning. "Hope and Patience are too young to take out somewhere. They haven't had their puppy shots yet and they could catch something from a strange dog."

I was not sure whether to be relieved or sorry. I wanted to protect the puppies, but by then I'd figured out that they would be something to talk about when I met the strangers for the first time.

"Maybe Rowan's friends can come here," he said. "Why don't you ask them to come over and see your tree house, too?"

"I can ask, maybe."

"There's no better way of getting acquainted than asking people to your house."

I wasn't ready to go that far yet, but I said, "I'll think about it." I was beginning to sound as weird as Rowan's parents, I thought.

"Good, good," Dad said, looking back at the map. The puppies, who had been sleeping on his old, cracked leather couch, woke up as if they knew we were discussing them and began crawling about. I took them downstairs with me.

"You're going to be a part of this family," I told them and I kissed them both on the tops of their smooth little heads.

Grady got home five minutes after Mom arrived, and I had a complete fit about the mess he'd left in the shower that morning. I hadn't told Mom yet, so she was an interested audience. Dad, attracted by the racket, came in and sat down to watch. The puppies lined up on the floor with Daisy, bright-eyed. They were learning to appreciate the show.

When I was done yelling, Mom said, "I think this bathroom situation is hopeless."

"Yes!" Grady said. "And it's Emily's fault."

"Ahem," Mom said. "Let's go straight to the solution. Emily gets the bathroom you two have been sharing. Grady can use the bathroom by the guest room."

"The shower in there is only two foot square!" Grady protested.

"Then you'll have to be careful with your elbows," Mom said. She opened the refrigerator and took out a bowl of leftovers. Dad rolled his eyes and Grady left the room, muttering something about girls and hair dryers.

"Thanks, Mom," I said. I took plates down from the cupboard and began to set the table.

"Don't congratulate yourself, Emily," Mom said. "I see your fine hand in this, too."

"I have more stuff than Grady!" I said. "I needed more space in the bathroom."

"You have more stuff than anybody," Dad said, siding with Mom. I could tell by the expression on his face that there wasn't a single thing I could do to come out of this looking as innocent as Hope and Patience.

But I had a bathroom all to myself! Unfortunately, so did Grady. He had lost and won, both at the same time.

Dinner was a rather silent affair. Afterward, Grady went straight up to his room to watch TV. I knew he was seething and blaming me for his getting into trouble again. Well, he'd have a big story to tell C.J. the next time he came over.

Rain had fallen again for a short while, so I opened the windows in my room to enjoy the scent of wet roses and grass. Daisy was downstairs watching TV with Mom and Dad, and Grady was still holed up in his bedroom, for once not playing his stereo loud enough to crack plates in the cupboards. I was beginning to feel guilty. Perhaps I shouldn't have made such a fuss about the bathroom. My brother would be living somewhere else in a few weeks, and I'd probably miss him. Not that I planned to admit it.

I leaned on the windowsill, appreciating my new yard even though the flower beds were overgrown, and wondering if I should put the rug and table in the tree house before it got dark. Then I noticed that one of the shades had been raised downstairs in Rowan's house. The light was on in the room behind, and I saw a man walk through it before the light clicked off.

That would be Rowan's father, I thought. Forget him, I told myself. My yard was too nice and I loved my new house. What else could matter? A light mist was gathering above the trees. The whole world seemed to be resting.

Suddenly I heard Rowan's voice, soft but clear, coming from her yard.

"But what did I do?" she asked someone.

I held my breath. Who was with her? No one answered her. "Talk to me," she said. "Please. At least tell me what I did." Silence.

"Dad, please," she said. "What did I do?"

I could see her now, between trees, facing someone wearing dark clothes.

"What did I do, Dad?" she asked again.

More silence.

I realized that my hands were clenched. I hated people who stopped speaking to someone in order to torment them. I had known a girl in sixth grade who treated everyone like that. We never knew for certain why Tory was angry, but she controlled nearly everyone with her pouting and sulking. I was the only one who told her that I didn't care if she sulked for the rest of her life because I didn't like her anyway. Of course, that happened before I lost my courage to speak up and defend myself. Before my accident.

Rowan's father gave her the silent treatment? So he would not tell her what, if anything, she had done to make him angry, but let her follow him around in the yard, begging him to answer her! What a dad!

Mr. Tucker, with his big black locked iron gates and his demands for silence and his insistence that the vacuum cleaner marks run parallel with the walls! How could Rowan stand him?

My family was tense at the moment, but we would get over it just as we always did. The Tucker family must be miserable most of the time, I decided. I understood Rowan's situation then—or at least I thought I did.

But it was much worse than I imagined. The worst of the Shepherd family problems were nowhere near the problems in the house behind us.

In Middle Dark that night, Daisy again woke our household with her barks and growls. I hushed her and pulled her away from the window but I wondered if what she heard that disturbed her so much came from the big, ugly Tucker house.

Daisy consoled herself by snuggling up to the puppies, which were awake and complaining with squeaks and whimpers. I sat on the floor with them for a long time, wondering what I could do to help Rowan. Maybe she needed someone to talk to, even though she hadn't known me very long. If she ever asked me what I'd do if my father stopped speaking to me, I'd tell her. I'd turn it back on him and ignore him until he gave up. Two can play at that stupid game.

But my dad would understand what I was doing. In my house, my opinion mattered.

Oh, brilliant, Emily, I told myself. With your luck, you'll solve all the world's problems and have a boyfriend by the time you're fifteen.

I had just figured something out. Your opinion mattered to your dad only if he wasn't mean.

Chapter 7

The next morning I changed clothes several times and worried about the impression I would make on Rowan's friends. If I'd had her phone number, I would have told her that something had come up and I couldn't meet her and the others at the park after all. Darn it! Why hadn't she given me her number!

I didn't want to go. Without the puppies, what would there be to talk about? Lorna and Carlene might ask me about my old school—maybe they even knew kids in that part of Seattle. Afterward, they might ask those kids about me. "Oh, you mean Ugly?" someone would say.

The puppies would have charmed Lorna and Carlene and they wouldn't have paid attention to me—or looked at me too closely. But Dad was right. The puppies needed their shots before they went out in public. And there was always the chance that one of Rowan's friends would have wanted one of the puppies and maybe even asked my parents for her.

I was going through all my clean clothes! First I'd put on shorts and a sleeveless T-shirt, then changed to jeans and a different T-shirt, and then I switched to a skirt and cotton blouse. Daisy had watched with what I was certain was a disgusted expression. Finally I changed back to shorts. They looked good. Sort of.

Of course there was always the possibility that Rowan wouldn't show up at the park. After what I'd heard the night before, I wouldn't have been surprised. Maybe Rowan had been grounded.

Then what? I'd go to the park and she wouldn't be there. Maybe she would have called her friends and told them not to go, either. But maybe she wouldn't call them, and wouldn't I look stupid, showing up all by myself, trying to find two girls I didn't know?

I was thinking in circles and getting nowhere. The best I could do was go ahead with the plan and hope it turned out all right. A new start was what I had wanted, and now I had it, for better or worse.

After breakfast, Dad took the bus to the university for a meeting, promising me that he would be home to baby-sit the puppies while I was gone. Part of me hoped he wouldn't make it back in time. Hope and Patience couldn't be left alone yet—they were too little. I'd have a perfect excuse for not leaving the house.

Dad was back by twelve-thirty. Oh well. I put on an extra layer of sunscreen to protect my face and hurried away from the house. I was so nervous that I didn't notice how overcast the sky had become, and I was a block away from home before I realized that I was chilly. Too late. What else could I do that was stupid?

I hoped I'd see Rowan walking toward the park, too, but she might have taken a different street. I checked my watch. I would arrive exactly on time, but by then I'd convinced myself that no one would show up. The path seemed as if it was a mile long. Overhead, the weak sunlight filtered through the trees and fell in patterns on the ground in front of me, and I found myself thinking about Rowan's whale, swimming beneath the surface of the water, her skin dappled with light. She wouldn't worry. She was safe forever with her mother and her friends, going and coming in a crystal sea.

What was it like for the pretty whale? What sounds did she hear? Did she play with other young whales? Did she leap out of the water and smash back into it, splashing her mother and all of her friends? Did she laugh?

I reminded myself to pay attention to where I was going. Maybe this meeting wouldn't be so bad after all. And Dad had been right about leaving the puppies home, because the park was full of children and many of them had dogs.

"Emily!"

Rowan was waiting at the pond with two other girls. I took a deep breath and smiled as she introduced me to Lorna Owen, a thin blond girl wearing a red sweatshirt, and Carlene Pearson, who had black curly hair that nearly reached her waist. Then Rowan realized that I didn't have the puppies with me.

"Oh, I wish you'd brought them!" she said. "I told Lorna and Carlene all about them."

I explained about the puppies not having their shots yet. Now was the time I could invite all three of them to come back to my house and see Hope and Patience there. Once, I could have done it easily, but I'd lost the knack of easy conversation with strangers.

———

"Can we go to your house to see them?" Carlene asked. What a relief! She was open and friendly and I was grateful that she saved me from trying to come up with an invitation.

"Sure," I said. "Let's go there."

"I love your house," Lorna said. She fell into step with me as we walked back to the sidewalk. "My grandmother is a friend of Mrs. Bonner's, and she took me there once, but that was a long time ago. I slid down the banister."

"You can slide down it again today, if you like," I told her.

Lorna and Carlene laughed, but Rowan was silent, and then I remembered that she wouldn't go inside my house. What should I do about that?

Maybe Lorna and Carlene would like to see the tree house. Rowan was comfortable there. Lorna dropped back to walk with Carlene, and both of them talked eagerly to Rowan. I gathered that they hadn't seen much of each other since school let out, and I wondered if they ever spent time at Rowan's house.

My unspoken question was answered by Carlene, who said, "Rowan, when can you come over again? It's been weeks. You come, too, Emily. We fix each other's hair and try on makeup. My parents don't care, as long as we have the mess cleaned up before they get home."

It appeared that I was making friends in spite of myself. But I wondered about Rowan. Could she only see friends if she sneaked around? I couldn't blame her, but I doubted if my parents would be crazy about the idea. Sneaking was definitely not on the family's list of acceptable behavior.

"What did I do, Dad?" Rowan had asked her father, and he had refused to answer. Was her mother like that, too?

Rain started falling when we were a block from my house. We began running, and I wondered if Rowan would go into my house if it were empty during the day and no one knew about it.

As if she had read my mind, she asked, "Emily, is your dad home?"

"Yes," I said. "He's baby-sitting the puppies, but he doesn't mind company. Anyway, we're going out to the tree house." There. That should make Rowan feel safe enough.

We had reached the corner nearest my house, and Rowan stopped. "I'd better go home first," she said quickly. "See you in the tree house."

She took off before anyone could ask her anything. She wasn't afraid of my father, was she? No one was!

"Hey, we're getting wet," Lorna said.

"Come on," I said, and we ran the rest of the way. Daisy greeted us at the door, yapping and turning in circles the way she always did when she met new people.

"There's the banister!" Lorna said. "Should I try it again?"

"Go ahead," I said. "I'd like to see you do it."

She shook her head. "Your father would think I'm crazy. Where is he? Where are the puppies?"

Dad chose the perfect moment to stroll down the hall, holding both puppies. They were awake and pleased to have company, squirming around ecstatically. Without being asked, Dad handed Hope to Lorna and Patience to Carlene.

I introduced everybody, but Lorna and Carlene didn't say much to Dad because the pups held everyone's attention. I didn't want the girls to get any ideas, though, so I said. "They're much too young to go to new homes."

"Where's Rowan?" Dad asked me. "Weren't you meeting her at the park, too?"

Lorna and Carlene exchanged a look. Quickly, I said. "She had to go home for a while." Then, before Dad could start a conversation with my guests, I added, "We're going out to the tree house."

"But it's raining," Dad said.

"The roof doesn't leak a bit," I said, and I led the way through the house to the back door and across the yard.

Rowan was already there, waiting for us, and Lorna and Carlene seemed to accept this odd behavior. The four of us just fit in the tree house, with two of us on each bench. Daisy, not wanting to be left out, curled up at our feet and Lorna and Carlene held the squirming puppies.

"I feel like I'm six years old again," Carlene said, looking around the tree house. "My play house was cute, but not as cute as this."

"Emily is getting a carpet and cushions for it," Rowan said.

"I've already got the carpet, and a little table, too," I said. "Even a tea set and a vase." We could have *been* six-year-olds.

Suddenly thunder roared overhead, and the rain poured down on the tree house. Daisy jumped up nervously, and when the thunder rolled over us again, she ran for the back porch. "I've got to let her in the house," I said. "She's afraid of storms."

I hurried after Daisy and let her into the kitchen. She scrabbled under the table, whining. I looked back through the open door and saw that strange flicker of blue and heard the loud crack that meant lightning had struck nearby.

Dad came into the kitchen, frowning. "I don't like the idea

of you girls being out there in the tree house in a storm like this," he said. "Better bring everybody inside."

I ran out and asked them to come in the house. To emphasize the reason, once again lightning and thunder struck at nearly the same time, much too close. Carlene and Lorna, carrying the puppies, tore for the back door, but Rowan hesitated on the tree house steps.

"It's okay, Rowan," I said. "Come inside."

She hesitated a moment longer, then said, "I can't," and ran for the fence instead.

I watched her, almost ready to call her back, but then I gave up and went back to the kitchen. Carlene and Lorna sat at the table, watching Dad tuck the puppies in their box, as if they'd known him forever.

"Rowan went home," I said.

Both girls glanced quickly at Dad, as if they were worried about what he'd think. "That's okay," Carlene said. "Maybe we'd better go, too."

Dad took the hint. "If you girls won't mind watching the pups, I'll go back to my books. I'm glad I met you and I hope you'll come again when the weather cooperates."

He left and I panicked. I had no idea what to do next. If Rowan had come in, I would have asked them if they were hungry or thirsty.

Mom had told me once never to ask people if they wanted something. Instead, offer them two choices, she'd said. That made everything easier. "Do you want milk or pop?" I asked.

They both seemed relieved. "I'll take milk, please," Lorna said. Carlene asked for pop. While I got out glasses, they talked about the remodeled kitchen, and I was glad to hear the compliments—and not have to say anything myself except "Thanks." I put cookies on a plate and set it in the middle of the table. The thunder had passed and Daisy came out to make sure that we knew how interested she was in those cookies.

"If the rain stops, maybe we can go back to the tree house," I said. "Maybe Rowan will come back."

"Probably not," Carlene said. She and Lorna exchanged another of those looks that I didn't really understand.

"She's nice," I said to fill the silence.

"She really is," Lorna said eagerly. "She's a wonderful artist. You should see her paintings."

"They're all of animals," Carlene said. "Animals and birds. And fish."

"She has them in her room?" I asked, wishing I could see them. It wasn't likely I ever would, though.

"No, they were at school," Carlene said.

Then I understood. Carlene and Lorna had never been inside her house either.

I drank my pop slowly while Carlene and Lorna talked about the new high school, and after a while, when the rain stopped, they got up to leave.

"Can I have your phone number?" Carlene asked. "I'll call you when we have our hair party and you can come, too. It's practically as good as a sleep-over."

"Every bit as good," Lorna said. "Except we promised that we would never dye our hair again without permission until we're sixteen." They looked at each other and laughed.

I wrote out my phone number for both of them and they

gave me theirs. I wanted to ask for Rowan's but I was afraid I wouldn't get it. They seemed protective of her.

But maybe they didn't know the number, either.

I waited on the front porch until they were out of sight and then I went back to the tree house to think over everything that had happened. The Queen's Beasts needed to be back on their freshly painted shelves where they belonged, so I brought in the box and put the carvings in place, hoping I got them in the right order.

But then I took the elephant back down and studied the smiling face. Rowan had called it Wide Awake, but then she told me about Lord Ganesha, the Remover of Obstacles. Which are you? I thought as I looked down at the carving. Wide Awake or Lord Ganesha?

It didn't matter. Any elephant could remove obstacles, and now the obstacle I wanted removed was Rowan's father.

No. I put the carving back on the shelf, ashamed of myself because wishes were for kids. Rowan's father was none of my business. Well, perhaps he was. He had been rude to Grady. Clearly he was mean to Rowan.

But then, she sneaked around. What would Mom and Dad do to me if I took off when they told me to stay home? They would ground me, of course. The grounding might be a long one if I did it more than once.

The truth of the matter was that I didn't know enough about Rowan to understand her situation. I liked her. She was lonely, so maybe when I knew her better, she would explain everything to me.

After I gave the puppies their afternoon feeding, I carried the rug out to the tree house and spread it on the floor. It looked exactly right, and the place seemed warmer because of it. I put the table in the corner and unpacked the tea set and vase. Better and better. All it needed for now was cushions. And the framed flowers Rowan had offered. As time went on, I'd think up more things to put out there.

"Hi. The place looks wonderful!"

Rowan startled me. I'd been thinking about the decorating magazines and I'd forgotten about her. She climbed the steps and handed me a bundle wrapped in an old towel. "Here. I hope you like them."

I unwrapped the four collections of flowers and leaves, covered with glass and framed in wood that had been painted red. "They're beautiful," I said. I remembered then that there were no flowers in her front yard. "Where did you get the flowers?"

"They're from my grandmother's garden in England," she said. "She helped me press them there."

"They must mean a lot to you. Maybe you shouldn't leave them here. Something might happen to them."

"She'll send me more, if I ask," she said. "They look just right here." She changed the subject skillfully and asked, "Did you like Lorna and Carlene?" I guess that we weren't supposed to talk about her grandmother very much either.

"Yes. It rained too hard to stay out here, so we had snacks in the kitchen. You should have come, too."

She looked out the window, then said, "That's all right."

"Dad wouldn't have minded."

Rowan studied her hands. Then she said, "If anyone ever asks him if I've been in your house, he can say no and be telling the truth."

I gaped at her, not believing what I'd heard. "But who would ask him something like that?" I blurted.

"My father."

I couldn't think of anything to say, but an ugly picture flashed in my imagination. I saw Mr. Tucker confronting my father on our front porch. I didn't want *that* to happen. We both sat there in a silence that was actually painful.

Then she said, "I've got to get home. I promised Mom I'd start the salad for dinner." And she was gone.

I didn't know her well enough to encourage her to explain why her father would ask Dad if she had been in the house. I guessed that he would be checking up on her because she had sneaked out. But what if there was something more to it? What if he didn't want her to have friends?

No, that didn't make sense. Did it?

There had been a time, when I was much younger, when I would have run into the house and asked Dad what he thought of all of this. But not any longer. I had learned, as everyone did, that parents don't always stop with answering questions. They might well have questions of their own, and often those questions were awkward.

I hadn't met Rowan's father and I already disliked him. I couldn't imagine what her mother was like. I had a strong hunch that my parents would be very unhappy if they knew what I knew.

But I liked her. And through her, I had met two other girls. If everything went right, I'd have a few friends when I started school in September. And nobody would know anything about me that I didn't want them to know. That was important.

Maybe Rowan felt the same way.

Rowan was back the next afternoon, and I brought a hammer and nails out to the tree house so we could hang the pressed flowers. We took our time deciding exactly where they should go and discussed our choices thoroughly. The tree house was worth the trouble.

"You'd think we were hanging Monet paintings," Rowan said, laughing.

I liked to see her happy and a little bit silly. It made it easier to forget about her father. I was ready to pound in the fourth nail when I heard the kitchen door slam, then Grady yell my name at the top of his lungs.

"I'm in the tree house!" I yelled back. To Rowan, I said, "That's my brother, Grady. Don't pay any attention to him. He's impossible."

But she had already started for the steps, ready to escape. Grady reached them first, however, and blocked her from leaving. It wasn't deliberate. He was just being Grady, oblivious to everything but himself.

"Oh, hi," he said to her in an offhand way, and she had no choice but to back up and sit down again. He ducked down to avoid bumping his head on the door frame and followed her inside, looked around, and said, "When are you going to grow up, Em?"

"What do you want?" I asked. "Why were you yelling? What are you doing home this early?"

"Where's Dad?" he countered. "I got off early and I want to ask him something."

"He's in the basement," I said. "What's going on?"

He didn't bother answering me and didn't wait to be introduced to Rowan, either, but started down the steps.

"Thanks for being everybody's idea of a perfect gentleman!" I yelled.

He turned around, looked blankly at me, then said, "Oh. Sorry."

"This is Rowan," I said crossly. "Rowan, this is Grady."

Rowan seemed to be speechless. Grady nodded, said, "Hi," and went back to the house. The door banged behind him. "Idiot!" I yelled furiously.

Rowan looked as if she had narrowly avoided a traffic accident.

"He's eighteen," I said, as if that would explain everything. But how could she understand? She didn't have a brother.

Rowan seemed to mull over what had happened. "So, do you two fight a lot?" she asked.

I considered this for a moment. "Sometimes we do," I said. "But I won't put up with anything from him. He likes to think he's boss because he's older, but he's kidding himself. As far as I'm concerned, if I'm right, I'm right. Grady isn't right very often."

I hammered in the nail and hung the picture. "What do you think?" I asked, meaning the picture.

But Rowan was still thinking about my brother. "What happens when you fight with him?" she asked.

It took me a moment to focus. "What happens? Like I said, when I'm right, then I'm right. Grady likes to tease and I hate it, so I make him quit or raise so much racket that our parents make him quit."

She looked at me as if I was speaking a foreign language. At first I thought that she didn't know much about anybody's brother, but then it seemed to me that it was more than that.

She didn't understand about my fighting back.

I almost said, "You know how it goes," but she didn't. I shrugged and said, "We fight and forget it. Sometimes I argue with my parents, too, but everything gets straightened out sooner or later."

"Lorna fights with her brother, too. But he's younger."

"Yes, well, families," I said vaguely. For a moment I'd been tempted to tell her about Grady and the mess he'd left in the bathroom we had shared, but I wasn't certain how she would react. My brother and I might sound like petty brats.

Rowan and I didn't seem to have the kind of relationship where people told each other their troubles. Anyway, did I really want to know? If she was sneaking over to my house, how long would it be before I got into trouble, too?

She took the unicorn down from the shelf and reached into her pocket for the knife. "I should work more on this little guy," she said.

"Where did you learn to carve?" I asked, relieved that the conversation had taken a new turn.

"My dad showed me how." She smiled down at her work. "I'll never be as good as he is, though."

So Mr. Tucker could be nice sometimes. I was surprised. I wanted to ask if he had taught her other things, too, but I had a feeling that woodcarving was it.

I felt as if I were watching someone who had only one good thing in her life, something given to her by her worst enemy. What sense did that make? I had trouble thinking of Mr. Tucker as artistic and I couldn't imagine him carving little wooden animals. That sounded more like something Dad would do.

I took a chance. "Does your father know about your Queen's Beasts?"

She raised her head and said, "No!"

She saw then that she had startled me, and she added, "They aren't very good. I wouldn't want him to see them." She paused again, then added, "He's what my mother calls a perfectionist."

If anyone else had told me that, I would have said, "Aren't all fathers?" But I didn't, because he wasn't like all fathers.

She worked on the unicorn for a while, talking about the other Beasts. In her imagination, each of them lived in a perfect place where they were always happy and always safe. The horse was one she had read about long before in the newspaper. She had been found old, alone, and abandoned in a muddy pasture, and a kind family kept her for the remaining months of her life as a companion to their young horse. "Summer," Rowan called her, because the horse was now in a place where summer never ended and the pastures were always green and full of wildflowers, and twenty other horses were there to keep her company.

"That's good," I said, forgetting for a moment that we were talking about an imaginary horse. "They're herd animals and aren't happy if they're alone."

Rowan looked up. "You know a lot about animals, don't you?"

"Not the things you know," I said. I almost added that I just knew the practical stuff.

It was easy to forget everything outside the tree house when Rowan was talking, and now I felt as if I could see into her imagination clearly.

After a while, she put away the unicorn, said, "See you later," and went home. I sat there for a long time, thinking of the last thing she'd said about the horse. "He's free," she'd said. "He can run anywhere he wants."

"We should be that lucky," I said.

"Just imagine it, then," she'd told me. "In your imagination you can do anything."

I remembered how I'd thought about the whale while I was walking to meet her in the park. In my imagination, I could escape what worried me. Did she do that, too?

Chapter 8

When I went back to the house, I heard Dad and Grady arguing in the hall. I stopped in the kitchen, hoping they hadn't heard me opening and closing the door,

"I don't care what the man wants for the car," Dad was saying. "You aren't getting one that's so expensive to maintain, now or in September. We laid out some guidelines, Grady, and you agreed with them."

"I *need* a car," Grady said. "I'd really like to have this one. Aren't you tired of me using yours to get back and forth to work every day? You have to take the bus if you want to go anywhere."

"We can always put a stop to that and *you* can take the bus instead of me," Dad said. "Don't pressure me. It won't get you anywhere."

Neither of them had seen me yet. I stood very still in the middle of the kitchen, breathing carefully, not sure of what I should do. I'd never heard them that angry with each other.

"Oh, thanks, Dad," Grady said bitterly. "You don't care if I have to beg to use a car. You and Mom told me you'd think about getting one this summer."

"That changed and you know why," Dad said. "You were warned not to go anywhere with C.J. if he'd been drinking, but you did it anyway. No car until you're in the dorm. And stay away from C.J. when he's been drinking."

Whoa! I thought. When did this business with C.J. happen? I wasn't surprised about C.J. drinking—he was such a jerk. What surprised me was Grady's going anywhere in C.J.'s car at a time like that! Drinking and driving ranked as a major crime in our parents' eyes.

"He *wasn't* drinking when he picked me up. That started later. What was I supposed to do?"

"How about calling us and asking for a ride home?" Dad said. "You knew that much when you were ten years old."

"You're *still* treating me like a ten-year-old!" Grady protested.

"The discussion is over," Dad said. "No car until September. If you keep this up, you won't get one then either."

"You promised!"

"You promised something, too."

"You're breaking your word. . . ."

"That's enough," Dad said quietly.

After that, I heard Grady stomping down the hall and up the stairs. Wow. Dad and Grady quarreled once in a while, but that was the worst yet. Grady knew all the family rules as well as I did. He'd gone past just trying out another new personality. He'd thrown away a chance for a car this summer. And all because of C.J.!

Dad went to the living room then, and after a few moments, I heard him playing the piano. He didn't play very often, even though he was the best musician in the family. I heard him fumble once or twice over the notes and then begin the piece over again. He was really upset.

Grady is crazy, I thought. Couldn't he tell when he was pushing Dad too far?

But then, did Rowan know when she was pushing her father too far? Was that the problem in her house? No. It was something different, something I didn't understand. That awful tension hummed along my bones and I shivered.

That evening Grady went to his room as soon as he finished eating. He didn't bother excusing himself. *Fine.* Now he didn't have any better manners than C.J.

Mom and Dad cleaned the kitchen, fed Hope and Patience, and turned on the TV in the living room. Both of them looked unhappy. There was so much stress in the house that Daisy sensed it and curled up under the piano, peering out at us like a lonely little stray.

I tried to read in my favorite living room chair, but I couldn't concentrate, so finally I gave up and went upstairs, too. Grady didn't make a sound in his room. I wondered what he was thinking. He had always been popular. There was no reason for him to waste his time with C.J., who was nothing more than a sly, manipulative brat with a smart mouth and a silly way of snickering that set my teeth on edge. Well, they wouldn't be hanging around together after September. C.J. had been turned down by the U and had enrolled in a community college. If they were in different schools, they'd lose track of each other.

At least, that was what I hoped, for both my brother and myself. The kids in my old school would forget all about me, right? Even if I ran into one of them somewhere . . .

I hoped that it would never happen.

The puppies were old enough now to pester Daisy mercilessly, gnawing on her ears with their sharp little milk teeth and crawling all over her as if she were a fur-covered pillow. They wouldn't settle down to sleep if she was around, so Mom and Dad took them to their room for the night, leaving Daisy with me. I read a book for a while, but I couldn't stop thinking about Dad and Grady. Finally I gathered up the decorating magazines and started through them again.

It was past midnight when I caught myself dozing over a magazine. Maybe I could sleep now. I turned out my bedside light. The room was stuffy, so I pushed back the curtains and opened the window. There was no wind, and the sky had cleared so I could see the half moon in the southern sky. The night was quiet and beautiful. I could imagine a unicorn in our yard, browsing in the flower beds and then raising his head to watch me as I watched him. Moonlight shone through the leaves and splashed on his silky back.

The lights were still on in Rowan's house so I wondered about her. Had she ever seen a unicorn in her backyard?

Suddenly Daisy leaped up and nearly knocked me over in her anxiety to reach the window. She whimpered and then growled, straining against my hands when I tried to pull her back.

Then I heard what she had been hearing. Rowan was crying, "Don't, Dad. Stop it! Leave her alone!"

A woman spoke, her voice too faint to hear, her words running rapidly together and ending on an inquiring, worried note.

Daisy barked sharply, but I shushed her and shoved her away from the window. She began whining again, and I grabbed her collar to restrain her.

I didn't hear anything else from Rowan's house and after a few moments, I wondered if I had imagined her voice. But Daisy hadn't imagined anything! She broke away from me, growling, and reared up with her front feet on the windowsill.

My heart was pounding so hard that I could feel it. What was going on in that ugly brick house beyond our fence?

Then Rowan shouted, "No, I won't! *You* stop it!"

I recognized her voice but I couldn't believe her tone. She sounded angry! Angry and perhaps frightened, too.

Daisy was growling so loudly that I was afraid she'd wake up Mom and Dad or the puppies, so I shut the window and pulled the curtains closed. For a long time I sat on the edge of my bed in the dark, biting my lip, trying to make up my mind about what I'd heard. Rowan was quarreling with someone, probably her father. The woman would be her mother. It was practically the middle of the night, so they must have been arguing for a long time.

Mom believed in intervention when there was trouble. She'd seen people in the emergency room who might not have been hurt if someone had intervened and helped them. She had told me a hundred times that if I saw or heard something that could mean people were in trouble, I should tell someone. Do something! she'd said over and over. Don't be like those people who watch out their windows while a neighbor is being harmed. Tell someone.

But *what* would I tell? That I heard Rowan cry, "Leave her alone"? Was I really sure about it? The noise had stopped after Rowan had shouted, "*You* stop it!"

I went back to the window and parted the curtains. Rowan's house was dark. The Tuckers appeared to have gone to bed.

Knowing Mom, who wasn't afraid of anything and didn't mind causing scenes if they were for a good purpose, she might call the police to investigate the noises I'd heard, even though she hadn't heard them herself. Then what would happen? Would the police go to Rowan's house, wake everybody up, and ask what was going on? Would they tell the Tuckers that I had heard Rowan shouting? That I had been eavesdropping late at night?

Rowan would hate me for embarrassing her. My parents would ask me a lot of questions about her. They would add the new incident to what had happened to Grady when he was mowing the lawn. My brother wouldn't be the only one whose friendship was being questioned.

I pulled my sheet up to my chin and shut my eyes. The problem at the Tucker house was over. Maybe it would never happen again. If Rowan confided in me, then I might *have* to make a decision, but for the time being, I'd be better off if I put the whole thing out of my mind.

But that awful feeling was singing along my nerves and I wondered if Rowan was awake, like me, and hiding behind her closed eyes.

Soon after breakfast Friday morning, Carlene called me and invited me to spend the day at her house.

"I'd like that," I told her, careful to sound enthusiastic but not so enthusiastic that I sounded desperate. "Are Lorna and Rowan coming, too?"

"Sure," she said. "Bring all your hair stuff when you come. We trade back and forth, too, and try out each other's things."

"Let me make sure Dad's going to be here to watch the puppies," I said. Hope and Patience were thriving, but we had all agreed that they shouldn't be left alone for very long. They had begun chewing on things and particularly liked the new carpet. Dad, who had answered the phone, had hung around openly eavesdropping, so I didn't have to repeat much of the conversation. He said he would watch the puppies, so I was free to go.

I thanked Carlene and told her I'd start for her house right away. "Yes!" I whispered as I ran upstairs, changed to a different shirt, and gathered up my shampoo, two different conditioners, my blow-dryer and rollers, the curling iron, and some sparkle gel that Mom had bought for us but we both hated. Who knows, I thought. The other girls might like trying it and maybe it would look better on their hair than it did on ours.

I had Carlene's address. She lived only six blocks away, so I kissed the puppies good-bye, waved to Dad, and took off with a full shopping bag. In the next block, I saw Rowan hurrying ahead of me, so I yelled at her to stop and wait until I caught up. While I was hurrying toward her, I wondered if she would show signs of being upset. Should I say something to her? Ask her if she's all right?

"Hi," she said, as if nothing had happened in her house the night before.

She was a better actor than I could have been. But maybe she'd had more practice. Dad and Grady had both looked as if they were still miserable that morning. How did Rowan do it?

"You've brought as much stuff as I have," I said. Her tote bag was full.

"Mom collects samples of things and gives them to me," she said. "I've always got more than I need."

I nearly asked if her mother knew she was going to Carlene's house but stopped as soon as my brain caught up with my mouth. It wasn't any of my business. This was what Mom had meant when she told me there was a fine line between minding our own business and intervening to help someone.

No, that's *not* what she had meant, I told myself. I knew exactly what she had been talking about. The problem was that I didn't actually *want* to know what was going on in Rowan's life. I liked her and she was fun, and if she was in trouble because she sneaked around—as she was probably doing again that morning—then I knew Mom and Dad would disapprove. They might view her as unfavorably as they did C.J.

I felt as if I was being squeezed between two rocks.

"How are the puppies?" Rowan asked.

"Noisy," I said, relieved to have something specific to talk about. "They're learning to bark, only it sounds more like 'Yap!' They pester Daisy all the time, chewing on her ears and barking right in her face."

"But she doesn't mind, does she?" Rowan asked.

"No, she's always good to them. But you can imagine how tired she gets—she's an old dog, after all. She likes having you around, though. Maybe you can come over and work on the Queen's Beasts again."

"Sure," she said cheerfully. "Next week sometime."

I guessed that her father was going to be out of town then, too.

Carlene's house was nearly as old as mine, but it was a little smaller. The kitchen was big, and that was where we spent most of our time. There was a large, wood-framed mirror hanging between one of the windows and the back door, so we had plenty of light. The counters had been cleared off, and we had room for all of the things we had brought with us.

We took turns washing our hair at the kitchen sink more than once, using each other's shampoos and conditioners. Rowan had a sample we all liked best, and everyone agreed that my sparkle gel belonged in the garbage.

Carlene dried my hair for me the last time, showing me a new trick with a brush that curled the ends under. Then Lorna sprayed my hair with something she called a "thickener" that her mother made herself. It worked, but it smelled awful, a little like sour milk.

"The smell goes away in an hour," she said earnestly.

"Thank you," I said, doing my best to sound grateful. "That's good to know.'

I was glad I was there with new friends. No one had said anything about the too-smooth skin on one side of my face and no one asked about my old school or any friends that I might have in another neighborhood. The closest anyone came to being inquisitive about my past was when Lorna asked me if I had a boyfriend. "Nope," I said. "How about you?"

"Whenever I start liking a boy, he usually tries to push me down or shove me into my locker, so maybe I don't have very good taste," Lorna said frankly.

"It's the age," Carlene said, "Mom says all boys are jerks until they're at least sixteen."

I thought of Grady and said, "Maybe they need to be older than that. My brother is eighteen and he's a pain."

"He's sure cute, though," Rowan said slowly, as if she was seriously considering this for the first time.

"I won't tell him you said so," I told her. I was tempted to talk about Grady's problems then, but I decided against it. Maybe everything would go better if I never told people anything negative about my family—or myself.

It was a wonderful day, and I was glad that Rowan hadn't been able to give up the tree house when the Bonners moved because otherwise I might not have met her and her friends until September, when school started. New beginnings were possible, I told myself. I just needed to be careful and keep Rowan's trouble to myself.

But Rowan was nothing like C.J. Maybe she was going to the tree house or Carlene's when she shouldn't, but she wasn't drinking like C.J. Probably her father was rotten and punished her too much for small things. And there was always the possibility she hadn't done anything at all and he was one of those parents who didn't want children to grow up. I was very careful not to think about what I had heard that night.

But trust Mom to be the one who would take on Mr. Tucker and start the second battle in the war.

When Mom got home from her hospital rounds Saturday morning, she told me she was ready to face a shopping trip, so we were going downtown to buy cushions for the tree house benches. We left Dad playing with Daisy and the puppies on the back lawn and Grady washing Dad's car in the driveway. My brother was actually humming as he slopped soapy water around, and when Mom told him where we were going, he asked if she was planning to get a small TV for the tree house.

He didn't sound serious, but I said, "No television. No computer. No music. It's a place to sit and talk."

He blinked, then nodded and said, "Yeah, girl stuff." But I wondered if maybe he didn't sound just a little sorry that guys his age couldn't sit and talk in a tree house themselves.

As we drove away, I hoped Grady and Dad would make up. I hated the tension in the house, and I was sure that everybody else felt the same way.

Mom and I still couldn't find the long narrow cushions I wanted, but in a downtown Seattle department store we saw square, red flowered pillows and we bought four of them, two for each bench. To celebrate our success, we had lunch in our favorite sandwich shop and then spent an hour in a bookstore.

"This is my reward for taking you shopping," Mom said as she headed for the mystery section.

At home, we put the pillows on the benches and tried them out by bouncing on them. Perfect.

"Did you think about what will happen to the tree house in winter?" Mom asked. "It'll be too damp then to leave the rug and cushions out here."

"The roof doesn't leak!"

"This place doesn't have a door," Mom said. "Or heat. I'm afraid you'll have to bring everything inside once the cold weather comes back."

I didn't want to think that far ahead. By that time I would have started a new school and Grady would have moved out. Everything would be different. Maybe I wouldn't like what would happen between now and autumn.

"Your bedroom is so big that I think you could put all this in a corner and you'd have a cozy place for you and your friends," Mom went on.

"Sure," I said. That sounded good. But Rowan wouldn't be there, not unless something changed at her house.

Mom had picked up the wooden whale Rowan had carved and was smiling down at it. "Look at this whale's face, Emily. Just look at that smile!"

"She's smiling because she's swimming back and forth between Mexico and the Arctic now, with no one around who can hurt her," I said. Then, seeing Mom's puzzled expression, I said, "Rowan carved this to honor a whale that was killed. A lot of the Queen's Beasts have stories like that, I guess. But she's just told me a few so far."

"And you want to hear more of them," Mom said. "I don't blame you for that. Maybe Rowan is like Scheherazade. What a gift."

"But you like her, don't you?" I asked. A small seed of worry was about to sprout in the back of my mind. If she knew . . .

"Of course I like her," Mom said. "Your dad and I were thinking about having an early dinner tomorrow, maybe at that restaurant on the waterfront we like so much. How about asking Rowan to go with us? Grady's going to a picnic with Melanie's family, but Rowan can get to know him better some other time."

Spending Sunday afternoon with Rowan and my parents would be fun, but I hesitated, blinking, while I tried to figure out how this could possibly work. I knew she couldn't go without her parents' permission. Since her father didn't like Grady, he probably didn't like the rest of us, either. Maybe Mr. Tucker would refuse to let Rowan go with us.

Their phone wasn't listed, so that meant somebody had to go to her house and ask if she could go. I felt sick, just thinking about it.

"Don't you want her to go?" Mom asked. I knew she had been puzzled by my silence.

"Yes, I do," I said hastily. "But . . . Mom, don't you remember when Dad and I walked over there to ask if she could go shopping with us? Their phone isn't listed, they have locks on their gates, and . . ."

Mom and I looked at each other soberly. "Okay, I forgot about that," Mom said. "But sooner or later we're going to meet the Tuckers, so why don't we make it today? I don't mind walking around to their house, and if the gates are still locked, then I'll just call out their name until somebody comes to the door."

"You would, too, wouldn't you?" I said, doing my best to laugh, but I was nervous, remembering Dad yelling "Tucker!" at the top of his lungs. "I'll call Carlene and ask if she knows Rowan's number. They're friends. She must have it."

Mom waited beside me in the kitchen while I phoned Carlene. I got their answering machine, so I just hung up, which was really rude but I'd never been so jittery. What if Mom ended up talking to Rowan's parents and they told her that Rowan couldn't go anywhere because she sneaked around? I should have remembered that before. Being friends with Rowan was complicated.

Mom was standing there waiting for the phone number, so I tried Lorna next, but her mother told me that she had gone swimming with her cousins.

"This is Lorna's friend, Emily," I told her. I took a deep breath then and asked if she knew Rowan Tucker's phone number.

There was a long, long pause. Feeling stupid, I said, "Hello?"

"I don't think Lorna has Rowan's number," she said gently. "No, I don't believe she has. But would you like me to have Lorna call you when she gets back?"

I said I would, although I was sorry I'd called by then. Something was wrong and I wasn't sure what it was. Didn't Rowan let any of her friends have her number?

I had to be careful how I explained this to Mom. When I

hung up, I said, "Lorna's mom doesn't know, but she'll have Lorna call me when she gets home."

"Hmm," Mom said. She tapped her fingers on the counter for a moment, then said, "Maybe I'll just run around to Rowan's house. That will be quicker. They might not lock the gates every day. Do you want to come with me?"

I didn't, but I didn't dare let Mom go by herself. She *really* would yell their name! We hurried around to the other side of the block and I grew more anxious with each step. This could work out perfectly, but it could also end up a complete disaster. Mom and Mr. Tucker seemed to me to be complete opposites and practically destined to be enemies. If Mom had heard what I'd heard coming from their house, we wouldn't be going anywhere near it.

When we got there, the gates were locked again. Mom stared at the house and hooked her thumbs in her pockets, never a good sign. "How strange," she said. "It's not that I didn't believe you, but . . . Well, I guess I'll have to call out to them."

"Mom, don't," I said, looking around. "Dad did that and nobody came out. Let's just forget it."

Mom's scowl told me she wasn't about to forget it. "I know what I'll do," she said. "I'll go home and write a note, then bring it back and stick it on the fence." She reached up and felt the tip of one of the black iron fence pickets. "Good grief. I could practically impale the notepaper on this. Who are they expecting, an invading army?"

I cleared my throat and said nervously, "It's probably part of a security system. Maybe their house has been broken into. Let's go home, Mom. The neighbors might be watching us."

Mom, who never worried about being watched, looked around and shrugged. "Maybe I should ask at one of these houses. . . ."

"No, let's go home and write the note," I said. By that time I didn't want to go out to dinner the next day and even if we did, I didn't want to bring Rowan. At that moment, her friendship was beginning to seem expensive.

But then I hated myself for thinking that. She had almost as much reason to wonder about being friends with me, after the argument that Grady had had with her father and then Dad yelling "Tucker!" loudly enough to be heard on another planet.

At the house, Mom wrote a note, put it in an envelope addressed to Mr. and Mrs. Tucker, and took a roll of tape out of a kitchen drawer. "Now I'll just run over and fasten this to the driveway gate."

"*I'll* do it, Mom," I said hastily.

"Why don't we walk back around the block together? Maybe somebody in the house will see us this time and come out."

No one did, though. Mom stuck the envelope to the driveway gate with tape and we walked back to our house in silence. I wondered what she was thinking. Her mouth was set in a line and she looked straight ahead.

The invitation had changed into a *test*. Mom was curious about the Tuckers now, and I was afraid she wouldn't give up until she learned what she could. I tried to remember that she was only acting like a parent who had a son who seemed determined to make and keep the wrong kind of friend.

———

Lorna called while I was helping Mom fix dinner. I'd answered the kitchen phone and as soon as I heard Lorna's voice I wished I had run down the hall to the living room phone. I could tell Mom was interested because she stopped chopping cabbage.

"I'm sorry I wasn't home when you called," Lorna said. "Mom said you wanted Rowan's phone number, but I don't have it and neither does Carlene. Her dad doesn't like people calling her."

I turned my back on Mom a little, even though I knew that it wouldn't prevent her from hearing me. "Okay, thanks for telling me, Lorna," I said, hoping she'd let the matter drop.

I was ready to say good-bye, but she broke in quickly, saying. "Were you going to ask her over to your house?"

Gosh, she was curious. "No, not that." Now I was embarrassed. Mom's plans hadn't included Lorna and Carlene and I didn't want to talk about inviting only Rowan to dinner with us.

But Lorna didn't wait for me to say anything more. "Her dad doesn't like her wasting time talking to her friends on the phone. Isn't that stupid? I can't stand him." Then she added quickly, "Sorry. I shouldn't have said that."

"You've met him?" I asked.

"At school, a couple of times. Rowan sang in the choir and her parents came to the performances in the auditorium, so she introduced us. He's . . . rude!"

That was for sure, I thought. I was tempted to tell Lorna about my family's experience with Mr. Tucker, but I knew better.

"How do people get in touch with Rowan?" I asked. That seemed to be a safe question, with Mom listening in.

"Oh, she calls us," she said. "I know she climbs the fence to stay in your tree house—she's always done that. But her dad doesn't know about it. He didn't like the people who lived in your house before."

He doesn't like us, either, I thought. "Thanks for calling me back, Lorna," I said. "I've got to help Mom with dinner now."

"Oh, sure," she said cheerfully. "Let's get together next week. I'd love to come back to the tree house and I know Carlene would."

I couldn't help smiling. "I'd like to have another good hair day at your house, too," I said.

After I hung up, Mom said, "I love seeing you happy again. It's been a while since I saw that big grin of yours. So did you get Rowan's phone number?"

She must have seen that I didn't write anything down! She was trying to pretend right now that everything was normal. What was I going to do? Admit Lorna didn't know Rowan's number? That would lead to all sorts of questions—but there was no way around it.

"She doesn't have it," I admitted. "Rowan's dad doesn't like her spending time on the phone."

Mom dropped cabbage into the salad bowl. "Some kids take advantage," she said without looking at me. "Maybe Rowan neglected her homework."

"Maybe," I said.

"Well, let's see if someone calls about the note," Mom said. "It will be nice if Rowan can come with us tomorrow."

"Sure," I said. The idea didn't sound so good to me anymore.

After dinner, Grady's girlfriend, Melanie, picked him up and they went out to a movie. Dad drove to the video store to get tapes for us to watch that evening, and Mom decided to go through her unpacked boxes to find the snapshots she had taken of the Queen's Beasts. I was flipping through TV channels when the front doorbell rang.

Daisy barked once, just to let me know she remembered her duties, and then she closed her eyes and snuggled up to the puppies again. I went to the door, swung it open, and immediately wished I had called upstairs for Mom to answer the bell.

The man who stood there wasn't very tall. His pale face was drawn into a scowl, and his almost colorless eyes bore holes in me. I knew without asking who he was, because he held Mom's envelope in his hand.

"Did you write this?" he demanded as he stuck the envelope in my face.

He made me furious! Without thinking, I snapped, "Do I look like Dr. Shepherd?"

I surprised him into hesitating, but then he shook the envelope angrily. "The note is signed Ellen Shepherd," he said.

"That's my mother," I said coldly. I knew even while I was sassing him back that he'd never let Rowan go with us now. Maybe I knew that he wouldn't have let her anyway, no matter how nice I'd been. There was something about him that got my back up like an angry cat's.

"How do you know Rowan?" he demanded.

What was I supposed to say? That Rowan climbed over our fence every chance she got to sit in my tree house? Now he had intimidated me, but only because I didn't want to get Rowan in trouble. Where was Mom?

"I'll get my mother," I said. "She's the one who wrote the note."

As I turned away from the door, he said, "I'm asking *you*."

"I'll get Mom," I said. "Wait out here." I shut the door in his face.

This was getting worse and worse.

I met Mom coming down when I started up the stairs. "Who's here?" she asked, scowling.

"The Bogeyman," I said.

She knew exactly who the Bogeyman was. She hurried past me to the front door. I trailed behind, both fascinated and horrified. Mom could be formidable. But Mr. Tucker would be, too.

Mom yanked open the door and snapped, "Are you Tucker?"

Oops, I thought. If I hadn't ruined any chance of bringing Rowan with us to dinner, Mom just did.

"Did you write this note?" Rowan's father asked. But then he made a mistake and didn't wait for her answer. Instead, he went right on, his voice rising. "How do you know Rowan? Has she come to this house?"

"No," Mom said, telling the truth. Rowan had never been in our house. "I know she lives behind us and I've invited her to go out to dinner with us. My daughter knows some of Rowan's friends. I take it that you are refusing our invitation."

"I don't want her going out with strangers," he said.

Mom was too quick for him. "Then I'm sure you wouldn't mind if she had dinner here at the house with us, tomorrow."

"She's not allowed in the homes of strangers," he said. "Don't leave messages on our gate again and tell your husband to stay away from my house. I don't like him yelling my name, and I won't put up with anyone mowing the lawn when I'm trying to work."

He turned his back and started down the porch steps. I saw him crumple Mom's note and toss it into our shrubbery.

Mom stepped out on the porch. "I don't know what your problem is—and *please* don't tell me—but you *don't* give the orders in this neighborhood, not anymore."

Then she came back in the hall and slammed the door hard enough to wake Hope and Patience.

"Jerk," she muttered. Then she laughed and said, "At least he doesn't know about the tree house."

"Hey, Mom," I said uncomfortably. Was she approving of Rowan's sneaking over the fence?

"Has she ever said anything to you about her father?"

I hesitated, then said, "Only that he doesn't want her going into people's houses. And she has to vacuum the carpet so that the marks are parallel with the wall."

Mom laughed, then quickly sobered. "The poor girl. Well, I guess tomorrow is off. Maybe I need to meet Rowan's mother."

"Don't, Mom," I said. "Don't go poking around, okay?"

Mom looked straight into my eyes. "Is there something else I should know, aside from the news that Rowan comes to the tree house without her parents' permission?"

I looked straight back and lied. "No," I said. "What should

there be? Rowan's father is a jerk, just like you said. Let's not make things harder for Rowan, okay?"

Mom sighed and said, "I suppose you're right. I should take a stand about Rowan sneaking over, but I'm beginning to suspect that too many people have taken too many stands with her. Let's say my memory is failing me. Least said, soonest mended."

"Isn't that something Dad says?" I asked.

"Yes, especially when I inquire about people who forget to take out the trash."

Dad came home then and Mom told him about our visitor. Dad shook his head and said, "If I can figure out when he's working at home the next time, I'll be sure to mow the lawn and maybe do a little work with my chain saw. Now let's watch a couple of movies. I don't even want to think about the Tuckers until I have to."

Sunday, the three of us went out to dinner without Rowan, but we didn't linger over our food. The puppies were old enough to leave for a couple of hours, but we didn't want to take chances. Even though we'd shut them up in the kitchen, where they would find fewer things to chew on, we didn't want them to be lonely for too long. "Are we spoiling them?" Dad asked as we were driving home.

"A little spoiling doesn't hurt," Mom said.

But nobody was spoiling Rowan.

Rowan came to the tree house Monday afternoon, bringing with her half a dozen cookies and two cans of pop. "I thought you'd like something cold to drink today," she said. "It's so hot! Oh, pillows! They're beautiful—and soft, too."

I had been reading, but I put the book aside and helped myself to a cookie. I wondered if her father had told her about our invitation—and the trouble that followed—and decided that he probably hadn't. Otherwise, wouldn't she have said something right away?

Rowan was wearing pretty yellow shorts, a dark blue T-shirt, and new white sneakers. Her hair was combed and tucked behind her ears, held in place by two silver clips. Lately she had looked so much neater than she had when I first met her. She smiled more, too.

"You don't go out in the sun much, do you?" she asked. "You have very light skin. I always tan but I get freckles."

I took another bite of cookie so I'd have a chance to think. I didn't want to explain about my accident and the surgery that left my skin too vulnerable to be exposed to much sunlight.

"Mom doesn't approve of suntans," I said. "Grady sneaks out to the beach without sunblock every once in a while, but he gets a lecture afterward."

"You have skin like my grandmother," Rowan said. "And light blue eyes like her, too."

"You miss her," I said. "Her and her cat."

Rowan laughed. "Do I ever! I wish Mom and I could go back."

"Are you planning another trip?" I asked.

She hesitated, then shook her head. "I guess not." She drank the last of her pop, reached for the unfinished unicorn carving, and took out her knife. "I should try to finish this."

"Mom's started looking for her snapshots of the Queen's Beasts, but she still has a lot of boxes to sort through. Would you see them again if you go back to England?"

"Gosh, I hope so," Rowan said. "It would be like visiting old friends."

"Maybe you could go by yourself after you finish high school."

"But Mom . . ." Rowan began. She shook her head. "I wouldn't want to go without Mom."

Dad came out of the house then, followed by Daisy and the puppies. He climbed the tree house steps and said, "Hello, Rowan. Didn't know you were here. Emily, didn't your mother tell you to take something out of the freezer?" He didn't look happy.

"I forgot!" I exclaimed. "I'll get it right now."

"It's too late," he said. "I was supposed to start dinner by now." He looked hot, tired, and irritated, and I was embarrassed both by my forgetfulness and his showing up to tell me about it when I had a guest.

"I'll fix dinner, Dad," I said, but I didn't get up. It was barely four o'clock and there was plenty of time to make sandwiches and a salad, good food for a hot day.

"Emily, you have responsibilities around here just like everyone else," Dad began.

"Dad, stop!" I exclaimed. He didn't need to nag me! "I said I'll fix dinner!"

Dad must have realized then that he was making a scene in front of Rowan. "Sorry," he mumbled. "Guess I'm grouchy because I don't like hot weather."

"Neither do we, Dad," I said patiently, letting him know that he wasn't the only person around who was tired of the heat.

He left without another word and I sighed. Then I glanced at Rowan and saw that she had turned pale under her tan. "Maybe I'd better go home," she said hoarsely.

"No, stay," I said. "Dad's bark is like Daisy's. Just noise. He won't bite anybody."

"But still," she said. "I should leave."

"Don't be afraid of my father," I said. "Hey, come on. Dad is a really nice guy." But even as I said it, I knew I was only making her feel worse. Even if she believed me—and there was no reason why she should—my dad was nice and hers was just what my mother had called him, a jerk.

Rowan settled down again, but she still looked doubtful. "Doesn't he get mad when you talk to him like that?"

"It wouldn't be right if he did," I said. "He was the one who was rude, coming in and talking to me like that in front of a guest. Everybody in the family knows better. Maybe he is hot and crabby today, but that's not an excuse. So is everybody else."

But Rowan didn't look convinced. She shook her head and didn't speak.

"Hey, look," I said. "Everybody is supposed to be polite to everybody else. That's the family rule. When somebody acts up, anybody else in the house has the right to complain."

Rowan let out the breath she'd been holding. "I guess," she said doubtfully.

Maybe she needed to tell her father when he was rude. But no, he was more than rude. Still, people needed to stick up for themselves. So that's what I said aloud. "People are supposed to stick up for themselves."

Rowan didn't look at me, but worked on the unicorn carefully. After a while we began talking about music and the bad moment was past. When she left, she said she'd come back when she could.

In the kitchen, Dad was making the salad, and he looked up from his work and said, "Sorry. I shouldn't have started in on you in front of Rowan. But you need to plan your time, just like the rest of us."

"I know, and I'm sorry," I said. I took plates down from the cupboard and began setting the table. "And I accept your apology for showing Rowan the dark, evil side of old man Shepherd."

He grinned and went back to work. We were friends again.

"Rowan asked me why I don't have a tan," I told Dad. "I didn't want to tell her about my accident so I said that Mom doesn't like us to be out in the sun very much."

"She doesn't," he said. "And you don't need to talk about your accident if you don't want to."

I folded napkins and set them on the table next to the plates. "I've never figured out if we're supposed to confide in people or not."

Dad sliced olives into the salad carefully. "There's no easy answer. Telling somebody won't necessarily make you feel better about what happened in the past. Dragging it up all over again just drags up the hurt, too. Is that what you're thinking?"

"Yes. But what about other people? If you see somebody

who might be in trouble, should you ask? If you can't come right out and ask, then should you tell something about yourself first, just to encourage them?"

"You mean like trading problems?" Dad said. "Is that what you want to do?"

"No! I just don't know if I should do something to encourage anybody to talk about things that might be wrong."

Dad covered the salad bowl and put it in the refrigerator. "Are you talking about someone in particular, Emily?"

"I was only wondering."

"Sharing a problem that's over with isn't as helpful to you as dropping it and going on with life."

I pulled out a chair and sat at the table. "Right. But what about the other person?"

Dad sat down across from me. "If this person asks for help, then you have an obligation. Otherwise respect her privacy. Maybe sharing problems only helps if there's something specific that can be done. Just complaining isn't a guarantee of feeling better."

"Then what are we supposed to do if we think that somebody might have a really bad problem?" I asked.

Dad sighed. "There isn't a single answer. Most serious questions don't have single answers. We're supposed to help when help is needed and mind our own business when it isn't." There was a small silence and then Dad said, "*Are* we talking about something—or somebody—in particular?"

If I told Dad about hearing Rowan's voice at night, then he'd tell Mom. What would she do? If she poked around in this,

Rowan wouldn't be my friend any longer. Lorna and Carlene would certainly take Rowan's side if Rowan became angry with me.

"No, nothing in particular," I said.

But he wasn't blind. He said, "Let someone take her own time in confiding in you. If you ask questions, she might say things she'd regret later. Even if she volunteers, you might still lose a friend. People don't always like to be reminded of their problems."

Would he say that if he had heard what I'd heard at night?

Chapter 10

Mom called to tell us she was going to be late, and she asked us to go ahead with dinner. Grady was late, too, but we didn't hear from him, so we decided to start anyway and carried our food out to the deck. The late afternoon seemed to grow hotter by the minute, but at least we had the illusion of comfort in the shade our big trees cast over us. Dad spread too much mayonnaise on his sandwich and grumbled about our not having air-conditioning in the house. I felt sorry for him and didn't remind him of what Mom had told him about loading up his sandwiches with calories.

I passed him the sliced tomatoes and said, "I know the heat is awful, but Mom said we never needed air-conditioning for more than two days each summer. The rain will start up again soon enough and then we can complain about that instead." I considered sharing my potato chips with the attentive puppies, but they didn't need junk food. Daisy assured me that she did, but I disappointed her and ate the last of them myself. She sighed and moved to Dad's side of the table. He could be talked into all kinds of things.

While our trees shaded the house from the sun, there was

no breeze. All the growing things seemed wilted. I didn't hear a sound except the next-door neighbor's sprinkler hissing out of sight beyond the fence. Apparently the birds were too hot to sing.

Dad sighed and poured another glass of lemonade. "Grady must have been miserable today. Outdoor work is hard when it's hot."

I almost felt sorry for my brother, until I thought of how much money he was making. I was sure he would rather have spent the summer the way C.J. was, hanging around and accomplishing nothing.

C.J. complained a lot, and so did Grady—lately, at least. Maybe my brother needed a tree house with his own Beasts. Perhaps he and C.J. would find something good to talk about then. Or perhaps Grady would spend more time with his nicer friends.

Had I just figured out the secret of the tree house? Did it set a mood? Did it change the people sitting in it? That was an idea I would have loved to discuss with Rowan, but maybe discussing it would change something. Talking about it could spoil the magic, so it wasn't worth the risk.

I cleared the table when Dad and I finished eating and mixed up the puppies' mush in the kitchen. They were eating by themselves now, and growing fatter and noisier every day.

Grady finally came home, red-faced and miserable. "What a rotten day," he muttered as he opened the refrigerator door. "I'm starving, but first I need something to drink. What have we got that's wet and cold?"

"Lemonade. That's what we had with dinner. Do you want sandwiches?"

"In a minute. Right now I'm too hot." He drank a whole glass of lemonade and then refilled it. "Where's Dad?"

"Reading the paper on the deck. Why? He's hot, too, so don't make him mad. Do *not* ask for the car."

Grady sighed. "I wasn't going to. I wasn't going to ask him for anything! Jeez, Emily, give me a break. Maybe I just wanted to see how he's feeling. I know how much he hates hot weather."

"Sorry!" I said. I'd been annoyed with Grady so much that I'd forgotten how much he really cared about Dad.

But Grady stomped out of the kitchen anyway and ran up the stairs. A moment later I heard water running in the pipes and knew he was taking a shower. And probably messing up his bathroom. But at least I had a brother. It made a difference, having a brother or a sister. If Rowan had a sibling, she'd have someone who shared what was happening to her.

Life could be much too complicated. For little kids, everything is black or white, fun or boring, good or bad. Now my world was filled with "maybes" and "buts."

Mom came home a few minutes later, while Grady was eating sandwiches in the kitchen. "The sandwiches look good," she said. "I'm glad Dad decided against fixing the chicken today."

I was tempted to take credit for the wise dinner choice, but told the truth instead. "I forgot to take it out of the freezer. Sorry."

"Fate," Dad said as he eyed Grady's sandwich with longing. "It's the foundation of civilization."

"I thought that was family meals, or maybe indoor plumbing," Grady said. He grinned and Dad grinned back.

We were okay again.

Daisy barked in Middle Dark, and the puppies woke up and cried. I turned on my light but I didn't go near the window. It was wide open and I could hear loud voices from the Tucker house. I couldn't make out the words, but I was sure it was Rowan and her father again. Good for you, girl, I thought. Tell him what you think—if that's what you're doing. And be careful.

The next day was even hotter. Dad spent the morning calling air-conditioning companies, and I spent the morning in the tree house, looking over the snapshots Mom had taken of England. She had finally found them the night before, along with a stack of guidebooks.

No wonder Rowan wanted to go back. What a beautiful place. I looked at photographs of castles and standing stones, men in red uniforms and ravens strutting on lush green grass. Several times I glanced out the window and hoped I'd see Rowan weaving her way toward me between the trees. None of the sights captured in the photographs would be new to her, but she might be able to tell me more about them. She had a way of making things sound magical.

She didn't come until the middle of the afternoon. I'd gone back to the house, eaten lunch, listened to Dad complain about how much air conditioners cost, and returned to the tree house with a dish of strawberries and a big drawing pad. I had just begun drawing Rowan's Queen's Beasts when she finally climbed the steps to the tree house. She was wearing a striped pink skirt, white shirt, and sandals. Her hair had been cut short and it curled around her ears. She looked great and I told her so.

She acted as if she didn't hear the compliment. "You didn't say you liked to draw," she said.

"I didn't tell you because I'm not very good. Today I'm trying to draw your Beasts."

She smiled at my drawing and then picked up the snapshots I'd left on the other bench. "Your mom found them! And guidebooks, too."

I erased a bad line in my drawing of the bear. "Look them over, and when you're done, you can tell me a story about this bear. I know there is one."

"I'll tell you now. She lives deep in the forest, where no one can find her and hurt her," she said. "She's very strong, but people shoot bears in the real world. Now she can spend forever and forever eating huckleberries and sleeping in safe places and dreaming good dreams."

In my mind, I could see the bear finding sweet berries in a sunny place and eating her fill, then napping in long grass. I wished I could draw well enough to put the scene on paper, but I wasn't talented like Rowan. I looked down at my drawing pad and sighed. "I wish I had your imagination," I said.

"I wish I had your *everything*," she said.

She caught me by surprise. For a moment my mind was blank, and then I understood what she had said. I almost sobbed, and I twisted away so she couldn't see my face.

I had good parents and a brother who wasn't *always* a pest.

I had pets. I had friends who were welcome in my house. She had a life in that brooding house with its ugly iron fence and a father who was more like an affliction than a parent.

Rowan had given me her wonderful stories and let me share her imagination, but there was nothing I could give her that mattered nearly as much. Finally I got hold of myself and held up my awful drawing. I cleared my throat and said, "Yeah, like you want all my artistic talent."

We were quiet for a while. She looked through the snapshots and guidebooks and I worked on my drawing. We became comfortable again, as we often were. She had enough to think about so that she didn't need to talk constantly, as some people did. In the past, I'd had friends who chattered endlessly, interrupting each other and talking over the top of each other. They could be exhausting, but I hadn't understood that until I met Rowan.

When I turned the page to begin another drawing, Rowan put down the snapshots and said, "I really want to see my grandmother in England. I'm trying to persuade Mom to take me back."

I jerked my head up to look at her. "You want to leave?" I asked. I must have sounded shocked, because she flushed.

"Well, people take *vacations*," she said mildly. "I'd like to see Gram and Libby again."

"And the Queen's Beasts," I said. My voice sounded too high. I had panicked and she must have known it. I couldn't blame her if she wanted to go away, all the way to England. "If you go, be sure to send me a postcard," I said quickly, to cover my uneasiness. I was about to add, "And let me know if you're coming back," but I was afraid of what she might say.

"I'll send you lots of cards, if I go," she said. She turned pages in another guidebook, and I tried to concentrate on drawing the elephant next.

After a while Rowan looked at her watch, then stacked the guidebooks beside her on the bench and got up. "I have to go home," she said. "Mom took the day off today. We got our hair cut this morning, and we're—"

She stopped talking suddenly, as if she had realized she was telling too much.

I blurted, "Your mom knows you're *here?*"

"Well, yes," she said. I thought for a moment that she might say something more, but she shook her head a little and her mouth drew into a tight line. When she started down the steps, she looked back and said, "I'll see you soon."

I watched her walk to the fence. She looked around her as if she were memorizing everything she saw. I felt a little sick.

She wasn't coming back.

Mom and Grady were both on time getting home that day, and we ate dinner outside again. Dad had set the sprinkler on the lawn, and a dozen small brown birds were showering in it, chirping and fluttering their wings. Daisy yawned, but the puppies watched, fascinated—from the safety of the deck.

Afterward, it was Grady's turn to clear the table, but he went inside and made a couple of phone calls. Sometimes he was good about doing his share of the chores, but sometimes he eased out of them so smoothly that nobody noticed he was gone until it was too late to call him back. Not this time! I looked for him to remind him.

I found him in the living room, and I heard him say, "Around seven-thirty, C.J."

I forgot all about reminding him it was his turn to clear the table. "You aren't supposed to go anywhere with him," I yelled.

Grady shot me a look over his shoulder. "See you later," he told C.J., and he hung up. "You aren't supposed to interrupt when someone is talking on the phone," he said. He was trying to get past me through the hall door but I blocked him.

"Maybe I should tell Mom and Dad you're going out with C.J. again."

"They never said I couldn't go somewhere with him," he said. "And none of this is any of your business, so butt out, Emily."

I longed to be a tattletale! He deserved it! C.J. wasn't going to stop drinking just because Grady couldn't ride in his car then. The two of them would lie about it, unless they were caught.

I *should* tell on my brother!

But maybe Grady deserved from me what I had given Rowan so easily. Silence. Why was life so confusing?

Grady stayed home that night, so either he had called C.J. back and told him he wasn't going or they had made plans for another night. I tried not to care. This was a situation that wouldn't improve because I was worrying about it. My parents could handle Grady, one way or another. I wandered into Dad's library and found a book about wild birds, and settled down on his old couch to read. Maybe we should begin feeding those little birds and encourage them to spend the winter with us. Maybe we could get a birdbath so they'd have water all the time. I'd talk to Dad about it.

Dad came in, peered over my shoulder at the book, and said, "What's on your mind?"

"I thought we could get a birdbath."

He groaned. "I suppose you'll only be satisfied with one made of ancient Roman mosaic stones."

"Wouldn't go with the house," I said, without looking up from the book.

Later, Mom and I were fixing our favorite ice cream dessert when she asked, "Did you see Rowan today?"

"Sure. She came over for a while and I showed her your snapshots of England and the guidebooks."

"How did she seem?" Mom asked innocently as she sliced bananas over the chocolate ice cream.

"Fine," I said, pretending that I didn't know what she was really asking. "She had on such a cute skirt, pink and white stripes. I wish I had one like it."

"She didn't seem like a girl who cared much about clothes," Mom said. "Maybe she's been watching you, my little clothes horse."

"Hey," I protested. "I've got more to wear than you, but so does Daisy."

"If dressing carefully is the mark of good mental health, then I guess you're in great shape," Mom said. "But where does that leave me? I never did believe all that stuff."

"You're a doctor," I said. "You're supposed to believe stuff like that." I handed her a bottle of chocolate sprinkles.

"Some people are eccentric about clothes," she said. "Like your father and me. Cleanliness is a better sign that the person is satisfied with life."

"Where does that leave Grady?" I asked as Mom covered the bananas with the sprinkles.

Mom laughed. "He's fine now. You're thinking of him when he was twelve."

I should say something, I thought. I should tell her right now that he's planning to go out with C.J. again. But they would let him anyway. They were counting on him to stay away from C.J. only *if* he'd been drinking.

"Speaking of bathing," I said, "I asked Dad to get us a birdbath. What do you think?"

"Sounds good to me," Mom said, licking her finger. "Do you hear the birds singing in the morning, before the alarm goes off? I love that sound."

No, I hadn't heard it. But I knew that Rowan would.

I knew just where to put the birdbath. Maybe we could get a couple of birdhouses, too. Then we'd have all kinds of birds here, singing and fluttering and watching us with their black shiny eyes.

I'd tell Rowan. If she didn't go away. But I felt as if a magical thread that connected us was being pulled so tight that it was about to snap.

Chapter 11

The breathless hot weather dragged on for another two days. The nights were too warm and we left all the upstairs windows open. Middle Dark was silent except for the occasional barking of a dog in the next block.

Rowan didn't come back, but on the third afternoon I found a note on one of the tree house benches. I was afraid of what it might say, so I unfolded the white paper slowly, as if that might somehow change the words I would read. Rowan wrote that she and her mother were leaving for England that afternoon at four. I looked at my watch. They were probably boarding the plane at that moment.

She didn't say how long they would be gone or when they were coming back. Or even *if* they were coming back. She promised to write to me, though. The last line of the note said, "Take care of my Beasts and remember me."

I looked up at the shelves and saw the Beasts looking down at me. Then I saw that the unicorn had been finished. It wore a necklace of rough flowers and it was smiling at me. I couldn't help but smile back. Somewhere the real unicorn was trotting through a field beside a stone cottage that was surrounded by flowers, and nearby there would be other unicorns that were always glad to see her, no matter what. Everyone was safe and happy in this world that I was learning to create by listening to Rowan.

I blinked and returned to the real world. I could see the Tucker house from the tree house window. It sat sulking in the blazing sun, and it represented Rowan's father to me, oppressive and mean-spirited. "I hate you," I told the house aloud.

I found Dad in his library and told him that Rowan had gone to England with her mother. I showed him the note. He read it thoughtfully and then said, "Why do I get the feeling that she isn't coming back?"

"That's what I thought, too," I said.

He returned the note to me and said, "Do you know why they left?"

"Her grandmother lives in England and Rowan really likes it there." I still didn't dare say more than that because I felt guilty. If I hadn't told him before about Rowan's problems, it was certainly too late at that moment.

"It sounds like they're leaving old Tucker behind," Dad said. "Did you know this was coming?"

I shook my head. "She only said that she hoped she and her mother could go back again." I added feebly, "Maybe it really is just a vacation."

"I hope so. She's a nice girl."

Hope and Patience were scrambling over my bare feet and I felt as if I were going to cry. I scooped them up and hugged them. "Dad, can't we keep them?"

Smoothly, without hesitating a second, he said, "That might be a very good idea. We've had enough good-byes for a while."

———

I didn't sleep much that first night. Several times I went to the window and looked at the Tucker house. A light was on upstairs, but the shade was down. I wanted to shout, "What did you do to them?"

Below me, the tree house was almost hidden among the dark trees. I'd still love it, even if I hadn't met Rowan there, but meeting her had changed me. Instead of slamming doors on my worries, I'd learned to look beyond them to places where everything was safe, and while I followed a whale or an elephant or a bear, I forgot about myself.

So is the magic still here? I wondered. While I watched, the unicorn came out from a shadowed place and tossed his head, inviting me to play.

The light in the Tucker house went out.

I called Carlene the next day and asked her if she knew Rowan had gone to England. I explained that Rowan had left me a note in the tree house.

"She left me a note, too," Carlene said. She sounded as upset as I was. "We found it on the front door. I guess she was in too much of a hurry to call and say good-bye. Anyway, Lorna got a note, too, but hers didn't say anything more than mine did."

"Did Rowan tell you when she'd be back?" Or if she's coming back, I added to myself.

"No," Carlene said. "Lorna thinks she won't." She hesitated a moment, then blurted, "It's Rowan's father, I bet! We always thought he was mean to her. He wouldn't let her talk on the

———

phone or meet a friend or invite anyone over to her house. He wasn't just rude to *us* when we ran into him after school programs. He was rude to her and her mother, too, right in front of us. He'd say things like, 'We don't have time to stand here talking. Come on, you two, stop wasting time. Let's get out of here right now.' It was embarrassing! Maybe her mother is getting a divorce."

I was tempted to tell her what I'd overheard coming from the Tucker house late at night, but I didn't. If I'd been Rowan, I would have wanted that kept secret. Added to what Carlene had just told me, everything looked even worse.

"I'm really going to miss her," I told Carlene. "She's been nice to me ever since I moved in."

"She's nice to everybody else, too," Carlene said. "She never complained about anything, not ever. Look, why don't you come over for a while? I'll call Lorna and we can have lunch here."

I checked with Dad and told Carlene I'd be right over. It would be strange, being there without Rowan. I felt guilty, having *her* friends as mine now.

Lorna arrived at Carlene's house at the same time I did, and she looked as sober and worried as I felt. Carlene led us through the house and out the back door, and we sat down at a picnic table under a broad tree loaded with hard-looking green cherries. A sprinkler ran on the lawn, with a rainbow glimmering in the spray. This place seemed cooler than mine did.

"Did you know that Rowan might leave?" Lorna asked.

"She told me she wanted to see her grandmother again. She didn't say she was going for sure or that it would be so soon."

"She talked about her grandmother a lot," Lorna said.

"Especially lately," Carlene added.

"She wanted to see her grandmother's cat, too," I told them. They laughed. "Oh, the cat!" Lorna said. "She told everybody about Libby. One of the paintings she did at school showed the cat sleeping on a windowsill next to a vase with a rose in it."

"She's probably there by now," I said. In my imagination, I saw a pretty house surrounded by flowers and rolling green fields and woods, and perhaps a unicorn or two. That was as different from the dark brick house where her father lived as summer is different from winter. It would be magical for Rowan, like the tree house was for me.

I learned from them that Rowan's mother was almost unknown and seldom heard from. Perhaps she wasn't allowed to accept phone calls, either, I thought. What a strange and terrible man Mr. Tucker was.

I stayed there for an hour, and it seemed to me that someone else was with us, someone no more material than a thought or a shadow. Perhaps, on the other side of the world, Rowan was imagining us.

June ended with rain, day after day, stretching to the Fourth of July and spoiling the backyard picnic we'd planned that included friends of our family. Grady's girlfriend came, along with three boys he knew. C.J. wasn't one of them—he had gone to Montana with his parents and his sister. We moved the picnic indoors, and we filled all the places at the big dining room table for the first time since we had moved in.

Everyone loved Hope and Patience, and I could confidently

tell them that we were keeping our sweet orphans. Melanie was disappointed with that, although she admitted that Grady had told her we wanted both of the puppies.

"He talks about Hope and Patience all the time," she said, as she scratched Hope's ears.

"No, he talks about *you* all the time," I said. She looked happy about that. I didn't exactly tell the truth, because Grady didn't talk about girls very much, but he had mentioned her several times, mostly comparing her hair to mine. I had to admit it—her long blond hair really was nicer.

Carlene and Lorna, sharing an umbrella, came by to have dessert with us, and we watched fireworks on TV together in my bedroom.

"Do you suppose Rowan was sorry to miss celebrating the Fourth of July?" I asked.

"It wouldn't be the first time," Carlene said. "Imagine celebrating *anything* in that house."

"Maybe she and her mother had a picnic with her grandmother," I said.

"Emily! I don't think the British would be interested in celebrating our Independence Day," Lorna said, laughing.

I felt really stupid and ended up laughing, too. "Maybe Rowan could celebrate her own personal Independence Day," I said. "At least she's with her grandmother."

"Yeah," Carlene said. "I'm glad for her, but I sure miss her."

All three of us sighed.

Two days later I received a postcard from Rowan, and the picture showed six of the Queen's Beasts. Rowan didn't write much, just that she hoped I was enjoying summer. Carlene called me an hour later and told me that she and Lorna had received cards, too.

"Did she say anything about coming home?" Carlene asked me.

"No. What did she tell you?"

"Just to have fun this summer," Carlene said. "Darn. Do you suppose she's staying there forever?"

"She's at least spending the whole summer there," I said.

"Is Mr. Tucker still living in the house?" Carlene asked.

Just hearing his name annoyed me. "I guess so. We heard his lawn mower running yesterday." I didn't add that Dad and Grady had joked about turning the hose on him.

C.J. came back in the middle of July and everything changed at our house again. I heard him kidding Grady about having to work "like a gravedigger" and never having any fun. The conversation was none of my business and I didn't want to hear it, but they were talking on the deck, right under my bedroom window. Finally I slammed my window shut, hoping Grady would interpret that as a hint to shut C.J. up. With luck, Grady might worry that I'd tell Dad how he'd been agreeing that he had a tough life.

After C.J. finally left, I found Grady and said, "Everything was nicer around here before C.J. came back."

Grady looked irritated at first, but then I saw that he had really *heard* me, because his expression faded and he almost looked embarrassed. "Not your business, sis," he said mildly.

"You were having lots of fun with your other friends, and they all have jobs, too," I went on.

I'd gone too far. "Since when did you start eavesdropping?" he asked. His face flushed and his eyes glinted.

"Hey!" I shouted. "All C.J. does is put you down. What's wrong with you? Why don't you dump him? He'd dump you fast enough if he could make friends on his own. Everybody hates him! I don't have to be blind to see that Melanie won't go out with you if C.J.'s around."

"Jeez, Emily, you've got a mouth on you!" he yelled.

"Too bad. Why don't you admit that you'd dump him if you could, only you don't know how. If you hang around with him long enough, it'll be your funeral."

It nearly was.

On the last Friday in July, Grady went out with C.J. He'd mentioned at dinner that he might see a movie that night, but he didn't offer any details, and Patience chose that moment to tip over the dogs' water pan, so Mom and Dad were suddenly too busy mopping up water and chasing puppies to ask Grady questions. I forgot about it and Mom and Dad must have forgotten, too.

I was watching TV in the living room after dinner when Grady walked out the front door. Mom came in from the kitchen and said, "Was that Grady?"

I didn't have an excuse for avoiding the question because I'd seen Grady walk out—and that wasn't all I'd seen. "He left, but he didn't say anything to me." I knew what was coming, and I already had a knot in my stomach.

"Who came for him?" she asked. "Melanie?"

"C.J.," I said. I *wanted* to tattle but at the same time I hated myself for doing it. Grady had been ignoring me since we'd had our big argument.

"Did they go in C.J.'s car?" Mom looked worried and a little angry.

I'd seen the car parked in the driveway, so I couldn't deny it. But I added, "Don't forget that C.J. is on his good behavior now." Grady was my brother, in spite of everything.

"C.J. on good behavior? Says who?" Mom said disgustedly.

"If you'd told Grady that he couldn't go out with C.J. *at all,* then you know he wouldn't," I said. That was true. Grady wouldn't openly defy our parents.

Mom sighed. "We've been trying to give Grady and C.J. a chance." She went upstairs to find Dad, and I knew they would worry. Everything had been much nicer during C.J.'s vacation.

Now Grady had undone everything with one stupid move. Had he done it because he was so mad at me?

I'd been reading in my room for an hour when Mom got the phone call from the hospital. Even before she had come upstairs, I'd had the same kind of funny feeling I got whenever Daisy began barking in Middle Dark.

Grady was in the emergency room, because C.J. had piled his car against a bulkhead.

"I'm coming to the hospital with you," I said as I got off the bed.

"No, you stay here," she said, already hurrying toward the stairs. "There won't be anything you can do."

"Mom!" I said. "I have to go with you!" I was sick with panic. The last words I'd had with my brother were angry. What if he was badly hurt? *Really* hurt?

She stopped at the head of the stairs, turned to look at me as if she hadn't taken a good look at me for a long time, and said, "Of course you do. I'm sorry."

I ran after her, and Dad drove us to the hospital where Grady lay unconscious. Mom and Dad were allowed in to see him, but the doctor made me wait in a small room with two other people who looked as if they were trying hard not to cry.

I hadn't thought to bring a book with me, so I tried to read a magazine. The print blurred, and I kept blinking. I looked at my watch a hundred times, and each time I checked it with the clock on the wall. What if something happened to Grady? What if all he remembered of me was my yelling at him?

A woman with a little girl came in, sat for a few minutes, and left again. I picked up another magazine and read the same paragraph over and over. I couldn't remember a word of it.

After a while, C.J.'s sister, Dilly, came in and sat opposite me. At first I thought she didn't recognize me, and I pretended she wasn't there for as long as I could. She had a pinched, pale face, and in the past, even when she had smiled she had made me nervous. She wasn't smiling now, and I knew her well enough to be sure she wasn't going to waste this chance to make someone else miserable.

I ignored her as long as I could, but finally I had to ac-knowledge to myself that she had been looking at me steadily, as if she was defying me to say something to her. I loathed her, and to make everything worse, her brother was responsible for Grady's being here. The two people waiting with us watched her staring at me, so I gave up and said, "Hi, Dilly. How is C.J.?"

She waited about ten seconds to answer, then smirked a little and said, "Oh, it's *you*. Mom's with C.J. right now. He's got a deep cut on his arm and had a lot of stitches."

She didn't ask about Grady, but continued looking at me with her head tilted to one side, as if I were on display in a store window. I wanted to get up and leave, but Mom had told me to wait right there. I picked up another magazine and stared blindly at the cover.

"I can see where your scar was, you know," Dilly said. I looked up at her, even though I knew better. The other two people glanced at me for a moment. "Boy, were you ugly," Dilly went on, apparently pleased with herself.

I couldn't believe she'd said that! Dilly smirked again and looked away innocently.

I don't have to put up with this, I thought furiously as I got to my feet. Her brother is responsible for my brother's injuries! Why should I sit here with Dilly gloating over me?

I went to the rest room, hoping she wouldn't follow me, and I splashed cold water on my face until I calmed down. The water felt so good. I let it run over my hands, and I thought of the whale, slipping through the ocean with her family, strong and quiet, safe forever. Dappled and smiling and peaceful.

When I went back out again, I saw Dilly's frazzled mother halfway down the hall, talking excitedly to a police officer and waving her hands. Dilly was standing behind her, listening sullenly to the conversation, hands in her pockets. The two people who had been sitting near me before were gone. I took the seat next to the magazine table and pretended to concentrate on an old magazine, hoping Dilly wouldn't come back. Where were my parents? Why wasn't someone telling me something?

After a while Dilly and her mother disappeared into a room at the other end of the hall. Now I could settle down to worry about my brother without wondering if I'd be attacked again. I thought of swimming with the whale and taking Grady with me through the endless brilliant ocean.

Finally Dad showed up and sat down next to me with a big sigh. He looked much older and very tired. "He'll be all right," he said, and I let out the breath I'd been holding since I first saw him coming. "He's got a concussion and a broken arm. He's in surgery now."

"Surgery!"

"It's a bad break. He was wearing his safety belt, so things could have been worse."

"And it's C.J.'s fault!" I said. "All he got was a cut on his arm!"

Dad rubbed his forehead as if his head ached. "He's in serious trouble. This isn't the first accident he's had when he was drinking."

"Maybe *now* Grady will dump him," I said, still angry.

"Growing up is a pain," Dad said. "I'm glad I figured that out a long time ago and decided not to do it."

I didn't want to laugh—how could anyone laugh on a night like that!—but I couldn't help myself. I poked Dad with my elbow and said, "I'm glad you decided not to do it, too. Maybe I'll be like you."

"Heaven forbid," Dad said. "Now here's the plan. Your mother is going to wait until Grady comes out of surgery, but I'm supposed to take you home."

"Not a chance," I said. "I'll wait with you. I want to be sure everything's okay."

He put his arm around my shoulder and squeezed me hard. "Good. I was counting on you."

Dad drove me home at two in the morning. Grady was all right but Mom was spending the rest of the night at the hospital. Our house looked strange when we pulled into the driveway. Most of the lights downstairs were still on. Did we live here? The evening had been so horrible that I'd almost forgotten our new home.

When we walked in the door, Daisy greeted us with hysterical barks, circling around us frantically. The puppies, who had been left loose downstairs in our anxiety to get to the hospital, looked up innocently from the shredded carpet where they had made their bed.

Dad stared at them soberly for a moment and then shook his head. Hope and Patience, proud of their accomplishments, scurried around excitedly. Then, to complete their welcome, both of them left puddles.

"Things could be worse," I said as I ran for a roll of paper towels.

"Yes, of course," Dad said. "The house could blow up." I could tell by the sound of his voice that he was only half joking.

On the following day I received a letter from Rowan. I didn't have time to read it then but took it with me to the hospital. We had to wait before we could see Grady, so I read the letter while I leaned against a wall. Rowan wrote that she was having a wonderful time with friends that she'd made the last time she had stayed with her grandmother. I felt a small pang but I brushed it off. Of course she had friends there. I had friends where I was now, too, thanks to her. I would share the letter with Carlene and Lorna.

Grady came home that afternoon, subdued and physically miserable. He had a large bruise on the side of his face and a cast on his right arm. He was right-handed so everything was hard for him. At dinner, Dad cut up his meat for him and none of us laughed when he spilled his milk.

"Here's my napkin," Mom and I said at the same time.

Grady sat there, looking down at the mess for a moment, and then he said, "No, just hand me a puppy."

The next day, while I was sitting in the tree house drawing, I looked out the window and saw that one of the shades in the Tucker house was up. Then I saw Rowan's father at the window, and he seemed to be looking straight at me.

I stared back at him while I remembered how rude he had been to Grady and to Mom, and how Rowan couldn't leave the house when he was home, and the way he wouldn't speak to her one time and yelled at her the next. I wondered what had been happening the night I heard Rowan shout, "Leave her alone!"

Didn't I know? Hadn't I always known?

Rowan's leaving had been his fault, yet there he was, still staying in the house. What kind of justice was that? Aren't the bad guys the ones who are supposed to leave?

He was still staring at me. Okay, I've got a message for *you,* I thought. Quickly I wrote some big words on my drawing pad and held it up to my window.

"I HATE YOU."

I watched while he looked, and then, to my enormous satisfaction, he yanked down the shade. Mom would have been proud of me.

I sat down again and looked at the Queen's Beasts. "So what do you guys think of that?" I asked them.

The bear seemed to be smiling a little wider than she had before.

Lucky bear. In her perfect world, she was moving around quietly in her forest, choosing which berries she liked best, perhaps digging for roots in the good places. Birds and squirrels would watch her, but in that place nothing would be afraid. In that place, everything was as it should be. Wind stirred the trees and the bear looked up for a moment, then continued on. There were exceptionally fine berries up ahead, and she would go there for the rest of the afternoon.

If I had never met Rowan, I wouldn't have known the magic of the Queen's Beasts and I would never have walked in that forest with the bear. Or slid through the water with my brother and the whales.

I was too big to cry, but I did.

Chapter 12

Grady couldn't work with the landscape company any longer because of his broken arm, so he and Dad played chess nearly every day on the shaded deck, drinking endless glasses of juice and eating the steady supply of sandwiches I produced. At first I'd thought that the long silences meant that they weren't getting along, but Dad finally explained that neither of them was very good and they both needed plenty of time to think up a move. They didn't talk about a car for Grady, at least not in my hearing.

Grady's friends—except for C.J.—came by the house nearly every evening, brought him videos to watch, and kept him up on all the news. Melanie baked cookies for him and admired my tree house—but didn't ask if she could sit inside. I liked her for that.

Carlene and Lorna developed crushes on Grady, which he didn't encourage, but I reminded them that he had a girlfriend already, one who was starting college with him in September.

"You're breaking my heart," Lorna told me. "He's the only boy I know who is taller than I am and isn't wearing braces."

"He's very old," I said. "Much too old for you guys."

"You can't blame us for thinking about it," Carlene said.

"School's practically ready to start, and we'll have classes with Goofy Jeffrey and his friend, Dingbat Sam. There's no hope for us."

"I can hardly wait to meet them," I said. I meant it, too.

Two weeks after the accident, C.J. came to see Grady. He pushed past Dad and walked into the hall the way he always did, just as if nothing had happened. I'd come in from the kitchen to see who was there, and when I saw him strut into the living room as if he'd been invited, I felt like dragging him back outside by his hair. Dad must have felt the same way, because he was scowling over the top of his glasses. The puppies ran after C.J.—they were willing to make friends with any-body—but Dad snatched them up and carried them out the back door. He didn't want just anybody touching them. Daisy ran along behind with her ears laid back.

Grady had been watching TV in the living room, and when he saw C.J., he said, "Hi." It sounded pretty flat, but C.J. wasn't the sensitive type, so he sat down opposite Grady in Dad's favorite chair.

I only moved as far as the piano alcove, where I sat on the bench and pretended to look through the music books. I meant to give them the impression that I planned to listen to every word. Grady didn't object, the way he once might have.

"How are you?" C.J. asked casually, as if my brother had been at home with nothing more than a cold. "Some of us got together last night for a party and everybody was asking about you. You know—whatever happened to poor Grady?"

"Everybody already knows about me," Grady said. His voice had an edge and he didn't look away from the TV.

"Yeah, *your* friends know," C.J. said, and his tone implied that there was something wrong with Grady's friends, who probably wouldn't have anything to do with him anymore. "I meant the *guys*." I could imagine what sort of *guys* he was talking about. Rich, spoiled, drunk, and arrogant. Trouble.

Grady turned his head then and looked straight at C.J. "How did you get here?" he asked. "Walk?"

"I'm using Mom's car," C.J. said, still at ease, apparently not picking up a single clue from Grady's tone of voice. "She knows I still need some way of getting around town. . . ."

"You don't have a driver's license anymore," Grady said pointedly. "You lost it, remember?"

"Oh, yeah, that," C.J. said, and he leaned back and smirked. "I told Mom that I thought you probably needed to get out of the house for a while, so how could she resist a good excuse like that?" He laughed, then sobered abruptly and added, "Dad and I had another blow-up. . . ."

"Who cares?" Grady said, and he turned his attention back to the TV.

C.J. said, "Hey!" as if he had never expected Grady to say something like that. Well, neither had I, but I managed to keep from laughing aloud.

I took advantage of the moment and jumped up from the piano bench. "Time for you to leave, C.J.," I announced sharply. "We've got plans. Good-bye."

There was a strange, drawn out moment when I wasn't certain that C.J. would leave, and I wondered what I could possibly do if he stayed. But he got up slowly and started toward the front hall. All he said was, "See you," to Grady, and Grady didn't answer. I closed the door behind C.J. a little harder than I meant to because I was afraid he'd change his mind. He was such a *spider,* and I didn't want him spinning any more webs for Grady.

Grady still didn't turn his attention away from the TV. I didn't know if he was really paying attention to it, but I left him alone and went outside with Dad and the dogs. My smile was a little too big to be tactful.

Dad was sitting on the bottom step watching the puppies wandering around the yard. "Is he gone?" he asked me.

"Grady wasn't very hospitable to C.J.," I said. "I don't think they're friends anymore. At least I hope not. Do you think this can last?"

Hope wandered close enough to Dad that he could pick her up. He cradled her in his lap and said, "Some people can only end a relationship if they find a reason to quarrel. It gives them the excuse they need to call it quits. That might be the excuse Grady has needed all along."

I thought about that for a moment. It made sense. "I think C.J. has always been jealous of Grady. He only wanted to hang around with him because Grady has better friends. Maybe Grady felt sorry for him. And maybe C.J. is so different from his other friends that Grady was curious. And it's hard to dump somebody."

"If I hear of a position in the psychology department at the university, I'll let you know," Dad said. "Friendship is a very complicated thing, but you seem to understand it better than some."

I didn't think so.

Hope had fallen asleep and Patience came looking for her, so Dad picked her up, too. Daisy, worn out from her responsibilities, curled up at my feet. I scratched her ear and said, "Aren't people ever just simply friends, *without* complications?"

Dad sighed. "There's an exchange of one kind or another that always goes on. People should become friends because they're good for each other. But the world has its manipulative C.J.s in it. And worse."

Poor Grady. C.J. wasn't good for him, not like Rowan was for me. If only I could have been that good for her.

To my surprise, Grady asked if he could come into the tree house one afternoon. When he got inside, he looked around the place approvingly. "It's nice in here. I didn't have much hope for it at first, but you did a good job of fixing it up."

"Why don't you sit down?" I asked, since he hadn't made fun of the tree house or of me. "The cushions are really comfortable."

Grady sat down gingerly on a bench. "I feel like an idiot," he said. "Sitting in a kid's playhouse."

"Idiots are allowed in here. This is a safety zone."

"You spent a lot of time here with that girl. What's her name? Rowan? You're too old to play with dolls anymore, so what were the two of you doing? Talking about guys, I bet."

"We never did," I said, and I was amazed at myself. "We

talked about all kinds of things—books and art and decorating and the Queen's Beasts."

"What?" Grady asked. "What Beasts?"

I pointed at the shelves. "Look at them. Those are Rowan's Queen's Beasts. She carved them and named them after some statues in England. Hers are different animals, though. And she has a great story for each one."

Grady studied the Beasts and then shook his head. "She's sort of a weird kid, isn't she?"

"Hey. She's not weird. She's just full of imagination, and she talks about things that other people probably only think about."

"Well, that figures. But she's pretty funny looking. I thought she was wearing somebody else's clothes when I saw her."

I had thought she had looked strange when I first met her, too. But after a while, she had dressed better, more like everyone else. She had changed her hair, too, and taken more care of it. What had she said? She wanted my *everything*. Maybe that included a lot of things—the tree house and our house, or maybe even my family and pets. And maybe simple things like an interest in clothes and hair. Maybe she even meant my big mouth.

"I wish she hadn't moved away," I said. "She gave me a lot to think about." A new thought registered with me then, and I said, "Maybe I gave her something to think about, too."

I spent a lot of time with Carlene and Lorna in August. Both of them liked to swim as much as I did, and we took the bus to the beach every other day. We had sleep-overs and shopped for clothes together, and twice we had lunch in the tree house. But there was always room for one more. There was always room for Rowan.

She sent all three of us postcards, but she didn't say anything except that she wished we could see where she was. So did we.

Late one afternoon, when I was reading a new book in the tree house, Mom came out with lemonade for both of us and sat down across from me. "I love being here," she said. "It makes me feel twenty years younger and not a bit tired. You've made this a perfect gem of a room."

"You're welcome anytime," I said. The lemonade was cold and I held the glass against my face for a moment. "It's awfully hot again, isn't it?"

"But fall's coming soon enough. You'll be starting school in a few more days. Are you looking forward to it?"

I finished my lemonade in a few big, icy gulps and said, "Yes. Are you surprised?"

"I knew you'd be glad to start school again after you began making friends. Will Rowan be back, do you think?"

"She hasn't said anything to any of us." I looked out the window toward the Tucker house. "Maybe she won't be back, especially if *he's* still there."

"The house looks empty to me," Mom said. She got up to look over my shoulder at the forbidding house for a moment. "But then, it always did look that way. Deserted. I wonder why nobody planted ivy around the walls to soften the appearance."

"It would take more than ivy," I said. Sometimes I had

thought that the house looked secretive, with the tall spiked fence and the drawn blinds. How would I change it if it were mine? I'd take down the fence and open the blinds and plant flowers and grow a tree so big that there would be room for a tree house in it.

Two days later, Lorna called me and said that her father had seen Mr. Tucker moving out of his house.

"Are you sure?" I asked. Laughing would have been tacky, but I was having a hard time not doing it. I imagined a huge elephant shoving Mr. Tucker's boxes down the street and trumpeting happily.

"Dad said he was loading stuff into his car and had a lot of clothes piled on the passenger seat. Just think about it! He's gone so maybe Rowan and her mother will come back now."

As she was talking, Grady came in with the mail and handed me a letter from England. "I don't believe this," I told Lorna. "I just got a letter from Rowan."

"Open it and tell me what it says!" Lorna insisted.

I put down the phone and opened the envelope. A snapshot fell out. There was Rowan, wearing a beautiful blue dress showing lots of bare, tanned shoulder, and her arm was around the waist of a woman who must have been her mother. Both of them were smiling. In the background was a flower garden in full bloom. I told Lorna about the snapshot and then unfolded the letter.

"She's coming back!" I yelled into the phone as I read. "She says she's coming back!"

Grady and Dad came into the kitchen to see what I was

yelling about. I was dancing around like a maniac, waving the letter and jabbering to Lorna. "Rowan is coming back!"

"Jeez," Grady grumbled. He helped himself to an apple from the fruit bowl and left again, but Dad sat down at the table and frankly eavesdropped on my conversation.

"The letter was sent days ago," I told Lorna. "Why does the mail take so long? She doesn't say exactly what day she'll get here, just that she's coming."

Within an hour, Lorna called back to say that she and Carlene had received letters and snapshots, too. "You'll see her first," Lorna said. "She lives right behind you."

And her dad is gone, I thought. Yes!

But then I felt ashamed of myself. It couldn't be easy, moving back to the house where they once had been a family. Even though Mr. Tucker seemed like a monster to me, he had taught Rowan to carve wooden animals. There must have been a time when he cared about her, if only a little.

Mom came home early for dinner, so I shared all the news with her while we set the table. Dad seemed as interested as Mom, but Grady's interest began and ended with the news that Mr. Tucker, his enemy, was gone.

"If I can ever mow the lawn again," he said, putting on his best "pitiful" face, "at least I won't have to put up with that idiot yelling orders over the fence and hosing me down."

"Oh, you'll be able to mow the lawn again," Dad assured him cheerfully. "Your injury isn't permanent, and I'm quite sure you can come home from the dorm and cut the grass as soon as you're able to drive a car."

I could tell by Grady's face that he'd heard *all* the messages in Dad's comment, too. He was almost ready to smile, but wisely changed his expression to cheerful indifference.

After dinner, I took my dessert out to the tree house, along with two new magazines that had come in the mail that day. I had hoped to see some activity at the Tucker house, but it looked the same as it always did, silent behind the blinds. Maybe Rowan would be home tomorrow or the next, I thought. Surely she would be home before school began.

I was halfway through one magazine when I heard someone come up the steps. I looked up, expecting Mom or Grady, but Rowan stood there, smiling and looking as if she'd grown taller.

I jumped to my feet. "Hey," I said. "You're back!"

She came in, glanced around at the Queen's Beasts, and sat down on the bench across the small room. "Everything looks the same in here as it did when I left," she said. "I hoped it would. Hey, I saw your new birdbath by the roses. It's beautiful. I like the plain cement ones best."

"Dad persuaded me that I had to give up my idea of having one made of marble," I said. "How've you been?" I asked as I sat down again. I had seen the stack of snapshots she carried, secured with a rubber band, and I could hardly wait to see them and hear the stories that went with them.

She was tanner than I thought anyone in England ever got, and she'd had her ears pierced and wore gold stud earrings. Her white jeans, a dark blue shirt, and sandals looked new.

"I'm fine," she said. "Just tired. I guess I've got jet lag." She hesitated a moment, frowned, then said, "My dad . . ."

I knew she didn't want to talk about her father or what had

happened, not today, and perhaps she never would. I didn't want to make her feel as if I believed I was entitled to an explanation, either.

"I know that he's gone now," I said, and I nodded once, hoping she'd understand that she didn't need to fill me in on the details. We could be friends without them. "Now tell me about your trip and show me those snapshots."

She took off the rubber band and handed me the first snapshot. "See the Beasts? I knew you'd want to look at them first. Oh, and here's a gargoyle on a rainspout. Look at his smile! When I looked up at him, I thought for a moment that he winked at me. I know that sounds silly, but he has such a friendly face. And here's the place where we had tea. . . ."

Friendship's dance. We had begun it again, and everything was all right now. Through the window, I saw that the blinds in Rowan's house had been raised.

The Beasts smiled down at us.

Epilogue

Before I went to bed that night, I examined my face in the mirror. At the end of summer, I was still pale. I leaned closer and touched my cheek where the scar had been. My skin felt soft, almost like velvet.

I could see my room reflected in the mirror behind me. What if I asked Mom for a soft bedspread, after I brought the tree house things in for the winter? A cream-colored spread, with matching bolsters.

No, it should be the color of the ocean surface when I looked up from a deep dive and saw the sunlight spangles. Or the color of a rich rain forest shimmering under a rainbow. Or huckleberry bushes at the edge of a sunny field.

I could see it in my imagination.

About the Author

Jean Thesman has written several award-winning novels for teenagers, most recently *Calling the Swan* and *The Other Ones*, which was named an ALA Best Book for Young Adults. She is a member of the Society of Children's Book Writers and Illustrators (SCBWI) and the Authors' Guild.

She lives in Washington State, the setting for almost all of her books.